Escape From
Tut Island:
The descendants

S. E. McKenzie

S. E. MCKENZIE

ISBN-10: 1928069215

ISBN-13:
978-1-928069-21-8

ESCAPE FROM TUT ISLAND

DEDICATION

To the generations yet to be born.

S. E. MCKENZIE

ESCAPE FROM TUT ISLAND

TABLE OF CONTENTS

TABLE OF CONTENTS 5
CHAPTER 1: THE DILEMMA 7
CHAPTER 2: 19
LAST LETTER FROM DANNY 19
CHAPTER 3: 23
MEN OF MILITARY MERIT 23
CHAPTER 4: 28
THE CITIZEN 28
CHAPTER 5: 30
RECYCLING DAY 30
CHAPTER 6: 34
THE RIGHTS OF MAN 34
IN THE NEW ORDER OF THINGS 34
CHAPTER 7: 37
THE DETAINER...37
CHAPTER 8: 44
THE LIQUIDATORS...44
CHAPTER 9: 47
THE GATHERING 47
CHAPTER 10: 62
RECYCLING DEPOT...62
CHAPTER 11: 77
THE OLD BOYS' CLUB.....................................77
CHAPTER 12: 84
CHRISTMAS LUNCH..84
CHAPTER 13: 105
THE MESSENGER..105
CHAPTER 14: 110
DISCOVERY 110
CHAPTER 15: 113
RESPONSE 113
CHAPTER 16: 115
CHANGE OF LIFE 115

CHAPTER 17: 117
WHERE IS THE BATTLE? 117
CHAPTER 18: 120
ANOTHER SHOCK 120
CHAPTER 19: 127
THE GUARD 127
CHAPTER 20: 130
1ST DAY AT MINISTRY OF PROTECTION 130
CHAPTER 21: 133
THE VICTOR'S JUSTICE 133
CHAPTER 22: 143
THE OATH 143
CHAPTER 23: 147
ANOTHER CHANGE OF LIFE 147
CHAPTER 24: 149
A WEDDING 149
CHAPTER 25: 151
ANOTHER WEDDING 151
CHAPTER 26: 154
ANOTHER HONEYMOON 154
CHAPTER 27: 158
GOING TO THE FAR SIDE OF THE MOON 158
CHAPTER 28: 161
AN ATTACK 161
CHAPTER 29: 165
ANOTHER ATTACK 165
CHAPTER 30: 167
DINNER WITH THE CAPTAIN 167
CHAPTER 31: 173
A SURPRISE ANNOUNCEMENT 173
COPYRIGHT © 2014 BY S. E. MCKENZIE 180

ESCAPE FROM TUT ISLAND

CHAPTER 1: THE DILEMMA

"I made a huge mistake not applying for the botman regiment. Last place I want to live, let alone die, is in this hellhole. I want to go home. I want my life back and I want to talk to another human being," Danny Parks said, trying not to scream into the microphone connected to the black box which was concealed under his armor.

"The rain is coming down in buckets and I can't think straight. My location is on the East Side portion of the combat zone. My body seems to be controlled by what looks like a flying gun. Running is futile even though I am being forced to run. I have no way to fight back.

If I have to die, I want to die fighting. I have no defense against this weapon. We were told that we would die as men of military merit; fighting. If I could only go back to my old life; I would savor every opportunity life had to offer. I haven't had a chance to live yet. Why should my faceless enemy bury me in his indifference to my life as if I were nothing more than cannon fodder? If I must run why can't I run towards something or someone who will shelter me from this fate chosen by my enemy?

How can I explain the loneliness I feel knowing my death means nothing to these people. The vibes of coldness and indifference surround me. In this world I am just cannon fodder. This world is manufactured out of hate and accusations. And trying to explain who I am just makes me appear to be a fool.

Here in this war zone, everyone is a casualty of war.

I wish with all my heart for some telepathic power which could direct my brother's heart to pull me towards him so I could share his life and escape my own fate. I am not ready to die; I haven't lived yet." As Danny spoke out words he was never planning to say, the strange flying gun continued to chase him down flooded streets in a foreign land. This land was called the Kingdom of Belunga.

"Today will not be my day to die, as long as my brother will let me in."

What remained of Danny was now floating amongst the stars, while Karl, Danny's twin brother, slept in his bed at home, located on Pleasant View Avenue in Pitville, on the other side of Earth.

"All living things are energy and mass. And as the mass reaches the speed of light, mass grows. Without energy the mass ceases to live and becomes part of the stillness of materialism and segregation, which I suppose is the process of death not life. As waves of energy surround me, I see a star in the night sky and it is showing me the way. I never wanted to die so alone," Danny's voice, still in the heavens, screamed out for what appeared to be the last time.

"I am a living man, and as long as you live in me, we will fight for the rights of man; you will always be more than just another spirit gone by. As infinity surrounds you, we as brothers, will never lose sight of our shared path, for you are welcome to live in me, for as long as I live.

Somewhere amongst never ending stars; light feeds light in constant motion, spinning, rotating, pulsating and always so alive. As stardust burns in the distance, look for the brightest star in the sky for it will show you the way. Even though your body is no more, and what is left of your spirit is now floating aimlessly amongst this stardust; the brightest star in the night sky is there to show you the way. Once you see the light shining on the path you must take, you will reach me and find a place for your spirit to rest. Together, as brothers, we will fight for the rights of man, until the day we die, as one," Karl Parks whispered before crashing onto the concrete floor while still holding onto his pillow with all his might.

Karl found opening his eyes difficult. Once awake, he was able to laugh at himself; he felt lighter and more flexible, he felt like a new man.

"And I will always stay true to myself. As a producer of the energy which I can call my own, I will remain in control of my destiny for as long as I live," Karl vowed to himself.

"Oh right, who am I kidding? I am living in the heart of the occupied zone. I only know freedom in my dreams," Karl said to himself.

Karl picked himself up from the floor. He climbed the ladder to his bed and retrieved his glasses just seconds before his com-corder phone rang.

"Hi Karl, it's Sue-Anne, have you heard anything from Danny? Is everything ok?"

"I knew it was you. I sure miss you. I haven't heard anything from or about Danny so I am assuming everything is ok. I had the weirdest dream about him though."

"Well you know what they say about twins. We will get together at the Golden Leaf Café on Christmas Day for lunch."

It was Monday morning. The siren blared as it did every day since the very first day of the occupation. It was time to listen to the reading of General Ono's Manifesto of Truth.

The siren blared for a second time. Karl and Sue-Anne were obligated to obey and had to do it in a hurry. It was forbidden not to.

"We better go, I love you Sue-Anne."

"I love you too Karl, see you Wednesday."

Karl closed his com-corder phone and logged into his computer and stood to attention.

"Good Morning Karl," said the sexy voice programmed into Karl's house computer.

"Good Morning Delta-C," Karl replied as the commotion coming from outside made it impossible for Karl to resist rushing to his window to have a look.

A Federation of Unity sponsored experimental Flying Spying Gun was chasing a small group of people who were wearing tattered clothes and carrying small bags of belongings.

Running from those flying guns was futile even though the guns were programmed to make the targets run. No one knew why. The guns were experimental. Karl could hear screams among the ruins in the lower part of Pleasant View Avenue. He wondered what would happen if the enemy was able to duplicate such a weapon.

"Please close the curtains, Karl. What you are seeing is upsetting you. Your blood pressure is increasing and your heart is beating rapidly. You are putting your health at risk therefore you must redirect your focus and energy," Delta-C instructed in a commanding tone.

The day began with the connecting of minds so that the citizens in district 2021 could be programmed to work as one.

General Ono ordered this to be so, day after day. To break this chain of thought was to show disrespect to the dead and wounded of the ongoing war effort. To disregard this order was to disrespect General Ono and his Manifesto of Truth.

While Karl drank his coffee he made a herculean effort to stay still. He needed to work but was being forced to listen to General Ono's words when those very words were making him feel hopeless and angry. If it wasn't for Sue-Anne, Karl would have nothing to live for. He hated being part of the anonymous mass which was obligated to follow the occupiers' orders blindly. It wasn't like there were sides to take anymore. It was really about layers, not sides. It was all about where you stood in the pile or more correctly it was all about how status shaped how long you had to kneel in front of those who occupied the layer above you. Nothing made sense anymore. It was as if the citizens of Tut Island gave up their ability to think for themselves so they could avoid being aware of their pain.

Tut Island was the perfect stepping stone for the Minese, since a constant supply of coal was needed to maintain its super power status. Tut Island was one of the last coal reserves left on the planet. Tut Island was the perfect island for the Minese to capture first, for it was located on the Pacific, and used to be a thriving tourist trap before the Middle East oil embargo took place against North America during the early 2070's.

The province to the east would be the next territory the Minese would try to capture. Deep, inside the province of Toil, were the greatest untouched oil sands in the world.

Tut Island was an island of two worlds. The southern world had been urbanized for almost an entire century, and the northern world was a land of coal mines scattered under bits of rock, mountains and farmland.

Karl was swamped with work. He didn't have time to listen to General Ono. As an accountant, he had to close his clients' accounts related to the year of 2075. He also needed to open new charts of accounts to prepare for the coming year of 2076. Karl yearned for a day where his routine would not be interrupted by General Ono's speech.

Even though, everyone was bored with the twenty year old occupation, including the occupiers; Karl was even more bored with General Ono's speech.

Karl did not want to go through life denying his own thoughts or living life as a fool. Besides that, Karl believed that he could write a better manifesto than General Ono's; a manifesto that would make sense.

The occupiers would always be foreigners to the older generations; the restrictions on freedom and movement would always be an annoyance to the younger generations. Nevertheless, the occupation was a means of protection from the even crueler force of poverty which plagued Tut Island before it became District 2021.

The draft was compulsory for most of the young men living under General Ono's rule. The cultural confusion related to who the enemy was didn't appear to bother most of the younger citizens as long as they were on the winning side.

One fact was perfectly clear; the Federation of Unity destroyed people more efficiently than any other military force on Earth.

The Minese used the power of algorithms when designing their Order of Things.

There were algorithms for everything. There was an algorithm which created poverty and one which created wealth. There was an algorithm which controlled traffic and an algorithm which controlled distribution of food and goods needed for maintenance of body and health.

Shortly after the Minese occupation of Tut Island, separation barriers were placed all around the old shopping districts of Pitville and Coalton, so that traffic could only flow to the shopping districts where goods from Mina were being sold.

Poverty was mind numbing and necessary, to keep the occupied weak and to inflate the value of Minese currency. The Federation of Unity's Central Bank of Mina channeled funds to wars and occupations all across the planet. The Minese bank depended on cash flows which were generated from all of the occupied territories, including Tut Island.

General Ono had supreme power over every organization related to Minese occupation including the Federation of Unity's Central Bank of Mina. General Ono had the authority to seal the fate of billions of people across the globe.

Like most young people, Danny wanted to be on the winning side. It only made sense.

ESCAPE FROM TUT ISLAND

Karl on the hand, wanted to live a life based on principles, primarily to protect the rights of man.

In this time of global conflict, most young men were drafted. Wanting to be on the winning side did not pose a moral conflict to most young men who were being used as cannon fodder by regimes all over the planet.

Not everyone believed there would be a better afterlife waiting.

The descendants of the elites gone by were defeated by General Ono, twenty years ago.

Liberation by the old school Alumni of Tut Island seemed very unlikely. District 2021 was becoming the most fortified island on Earth. Even Danny accepted his fate when drafted. Danny said he was on the winning side, which was the best side to be on.

The Federation of Unity's anthem played in the background. Karl knew the words in his own language for they were hanging on the wall in an Eframe. Karl had no idea how to sing the anthem in the Minese language so he didn't even try. He couldn't speak Minese, he couldn't read Minese and he couldn't write Minese. It was the law that no one but the Minese could be educated in Minese.

As the anthem played, Karl rose for the 21 gun salute, in honor of the fallen, from the day before.

Every day, civilians, who were not eligible to participate in the war physically, were obligated to participate in the war psychologically.

Every day, the morning memorial service was filmed at random locations, known only to a few.

Gloves, beret and boots were carefully placed on the Minese flag, which covered the coffin of the Unknown Soldier. These items were no longer given to the next of kin but were returned to the stockroom.

Sentimental tasks were now too complicated and expensive to be eligible, even though still qualified, for public funding. The end was near and a new beginning was in sight to all who shared General Ono's vision. Karl couldn't differentiate between what was ending and what was beginning and believed that the whole argument defied common sense.

The Manifesto of Truth claimed that all surplus money was being used to win the war; win the war for whom, was always the question that few had the courage to ask.

Karl believed that the war was really between various members of the dictator class; squabbling amongst themselves while using ordinary people as pawns. The more intense this squabble became, the higher the price the pawns would have to pay; if the war didn't kill them first.

General Ono's Manifesto of Truth was broadcasted throughout the Federation of Unity several times a day in the local dialect. The document was thousands of pages long and was revised almost daily in local dialect.

"The fiscal goals for 2075 have not been met. Every day we live, we must contribute to the paying down of District 2021's debt. The war for Unity cannot be lost," General Ono droned in the background.

Karl had lived under General Ono's occupation for as long as he could remember. The occupation, which destroyed so many lives of the older generations, didn't feel foreign to Karl's generation. Karl had always lived under the occupation. He was used to the world of closed doors that only the right body chip could open.

District 2021 was not only occupied by the Minese, it was legally indebted to the Federation of Unity's Central Bank of Mina.

If the district's debt was paid off while Karl was still alive, he might have the means and chance to leave the island permanently without being required by law to return.

Where would Karl go? He had no idea. He wanted to find a place where he could be happy and raise his family in peace.

ESCAPE FROM TUT ISLAND

Karl was one of the privileged few who was allowed to leave the district for a short vacation mostly because Danny was one of General Ono's prized new recruits. Any unauthorized exit would lead to being hunted down, like an animal. This reality only mattered when he took the time to think about it.

There were thousands of failed states, losers from past wars. All these states were now under the Federation of Unity's jurisdiction where financial and spiritual unities were compulsory. These districts were assigned numbers by Unity officials and were identified with nothing more than their District's Identification Number.

The memorial service was now complete. Karl felt incredibly lonely in a primal sort of way. Maybe if he didn't feel so anxious his pain would be less intense.

The reading from the Manifesto of Truth was about to begin, and Karl was forced to sit and listen while his work was piling up.

General Ono was General in Chief and was referred to as the Supreme One. He was in charge of all the districts which fell under the Federation of Unity's jurisdiction and controlled by the Central Bank of Mina.

General Ono led the Service of Unity every morning from an unknown location.

"Today, even during this holiday season, we honor those who have made the greatest sacrifice of all. In time, the ending to their life will bring new beginnings and opportunities."

Karl wanted to work; not waste his time listening to General Ono's Manifesto of Truth and war propaganda. He fumbled through his organizer realizing it was impossible to follow General Ono's words and work at the same time.

Karl believed it was his duty to find a way for his clients to maintain solvency; because true wealth, he believed, was not about numbers; it was about people.

Karl bowed his head slightly as he watched the second part of the ceremony, which usually left him disturbed for the rest of the day. The story never changed. War implied violence. War was dictated by mostly old men praising young men for being too eager to die before giving themselves a chance to live.

As General Ono recited his speech a roar could be heard in the background. Karl raised his head for a moment and heard a second roar.

Karl felt a sense of hope as he realized that the secret place where General Ono was broadcasting from might be under attack.

General Ono held onto the microphone to prevent it from shaking. The coffin was still in public view, like similar coffins were every morning, but this was the first time the beret and boots actually fell from the coffin onto the floor.

The broadcast continued, while two young cadets marched to where the beret and boots fell. As the children were about to pick up the items from the floor, there was a third roar which shook the coffin until the nails could not hold any longer. The lid popped open, sending the children running out of the room screaming.

All was silent until a pleasant female voice explained that due to technical difficulties, the morning reading from the Manifesto of Truth would continue in a few moments.

Even though rather chilling, Karl found this whole episode uplifting. In the greater cycle of things beyond the occupation, young men from all over the world, would be demanding their independence so they could become who they wanted to be, not who they were told to be. Possibly the Unknown Soldier in the coffin was doing the same.

Once the 'technical difficulty' had been corrected, General Ono continued the reading of his Manifesto of Truth.

ESCAPE FROM TUT ISLAND

"We know how the powers of creation and destruction are in constant struggle to dominate. I, General Ono, will help you balance these two forces."

Karl wished for a speech which would stress independence of the individual and a bit of common sense. General Ono was the occupier and the occupied feared him. The younger generation, born into the occupation, only knew occupation.

Years ago, memorial services were private, with private chaplains. Ever since District 2021 lost the last war, such private services were a distant memory, retold once in a while, by the remaining community elders.

Karl poured himself a cup of coffee, missed the cup, and spilled it all over himself. He couldn't just leave the room to clean up. He had to get permission from his computer.

Karl tried following what General Ono was saying.

One of the functions of General Ono's speech was to remind all the citizens of District 2021 what was owed to the Federation of Unity's Central Bank of Mina. Today was no different.

Karl's back ached. He stretched his back and tried to follow the words General Ono was saying. The daily ritual listening to the reading of General Ono's Manifesto of Truth was mind numbing.

"We must never let go of what we know to be true. Only together will we find a way to regain Earth's balance. Our lives and survival as a species depend on our ability and willingness to lighten the growing dead weight, found on the other side of Earth. This is not war, this is unity. We must not only cherish our unity and common thoughts; we must be willing to sacrifice for the greater good.

We must work together to lessen the weight on the other side of Earth. As Earth's ice melts, Earth's tilt increases. We must prepare for the extremes of the seasons.

The coming period of darkness will be long," General Ono said in a practiced drawl.

Karl stared at his screen. What General Ono was saying did not make sense. He wondered if there was a chance that the forces from the outside were getting ready to liberate Tut Island from the Minese occupation, which was the only form of government he had ever known. Karl, like most from his generation, wasn't sure where he fit into the scheme of things. Danny always wanted to be on the winning side, but Karl wanted to be on the side which respected the natural rights of man. Karl wanted to live in a society where he would be better off than he would be if he was just surviving in Nature's Fields.

"Was a liberation force on its way?" Karl wondered to himself.

CHAPTER 2:
LAST LETTER FROM DANNY

A few hours had gone by. Loud knocking jolted Karl from another dream of flying through a sky of stardust where the brightest star was pointing to a direction which seemed to be leading to the emptiness of infinity.

As Karl stood up, he felt less certain of what was yet to come.

With a struggle, he lifted himself from the overstuffed chair, realizing that he had been asleep for a while; he didn't know what the time was.

Karl tilted his head as he looked through the peephole. The smiling mailman was waving a legal sized envelope in front of the door and holding an umbrella with the other hand. Karl's heart sank. He struggled to slide the rusty bolt to the open position. This mail carrier was about to fulfill Karl's worst fears.

Mail carriers were fate's messengers. Every letter that a mail carrier had in his sack would become a true representation of what fate was about to throw in the face of the receiver, often being the only notice.

"What an incredible day it is today," George said loudly so he could be heard as both he and Karl struggled with the door knob before he entered Karl's house and gave him the letter.

"Thank you," Karl said hoping that he would not have to engage in small talk with George. Whatever was in the mail was going to be bad news. Karl signed his name as quickly as he could. As soon as George gave him the envelope he closed the door.

Karl opened the envelope. He had no idea who B & B llP was and the wording of the letter only confused him further.

Enclosed in the letter, was a list of Danny's personal effects that he bequeathed to Karl.

"Oh Danny, you kept your promise," Karl said to himself in a whisper as he unfolded the certificate of ownership of the very lunar property they both fought over as boys.

"You are a man of military merit, now," was written on a sympathy card.

Karl's head throbbed as he remembered the day, though a decade ago, when Danny pushed him out of the way, as their father held out two certificates proving ownership of the two moon properties, one on the near side of the moon, the other on the far side. Karl was left with the far side property and blood gushing from the wound to his forehead. Karl knew it wasn't Danny's fault that he fell on the coffee table. Karl wanted the near side property just as much as his brother did, but he would have never used force to get it, it wasn't his way.

Today, he would have given both properties back to his brother in a heartbeat, if he could only have one more chance to argue with him just like old times.

Karl opened another small envelope; inside were two letters. One was the official letter from the lawyers. The second letter was a letter Danny wrote in case he was killed in battle. Karl held Danny's letter close to his heart; inside the second envelope he found two tickets to the moon, and a debit card to Danny's bank account holding money he had saved over the years.

ESCAPE FROM TUT ISLAND

Karl found Danny's last letter hard to read.

Hi Karl:
I guess if you are reading this, I am dead and you now
have power of attorney over all my worldly
possessions. I suppose you must be grief stricken. I
don't know why though, all we did was fight. Please
be kind to Sue-Anne, no matter what, please show her
all the love we both feel for her. Love her as if you are
two men of merit. Enjoy the rest of your lives together.
Obviously your life is already longer than mine.
Regards,
Your twin brother,
Lieutenant Danny Parks.

Karl climbed the ladder to his bed forgetting rule 2021. Karl was either getting the rules mixed up or forgetting them entirely. Karl's house computer never forgot rules. Delta-C announced rule 2021 had been broken. Karl tried to erase the log the way he used to do, but today the log would not erase.

Karl cursed the robotic voice and the present day order of things. He wished for a real voice that would speak kind words to him. He wouldn't even care what it said, as long as the voice was real and sincere. Everything around him was manufactured and was unable to respond beyond a programmed loop, the way a living thing could choose to do.

Unlike rules, no one cared when dreams were broken. Most of Karl's dreams had been broken a long time ago. Danny and Karl were planning to go to the moon together. Karl's doubting began to torment his mind. He tilted his head and fumbled for the bottle of pills in his pocket.

He took a pill out of the bottle and began to chew it until it dissolved in his mouth. Its effect would soon hit him and he would no longer feel so anxious.

CHAPTER 3:
MEN OF MILITARY MERIT

It was Tuesday morning and Christmas Eve. Karl had just finished hanging Danny's transformation certificate and Green Badge for Military Merit beside Karl's father's transformation certificate.

Karl watched as the two seals changed color in unison. The seals were very beautiful.

There would be no private funeral. There was no time for such sentimentalities. There was a mass service for the War Dead every day. Anyone who had lost loved ones just had to remember them in their own way. Many bodies would never be recovered. And even if they were found, where would they put them all? By 2075, there were just too many dead heroes to bury them all. How many fields could actually be filled with millions of crosses without effecting food production? Land was so expensive because it was the foundation for life.

To General Ono the solution was clear; one dead hero and his cross could represent a million dead heroes. This solution was not just practical but it could bring unity in anonymity, which was the core principle of representative democracy defined by the Federation of Unity which was proudly sponsored by the Central Bank of Mina. This policy was accepted by most people accept Karl, since like most of General Ono's policies; they never made sense to Karl. All of General Ono's policies depended on a polite deference to all authority.

One important question was being left unanswered; where did all the War Dead go, if they were not chosen to be the representative of one million other dead soldiers?

Not having a personalized funeral service, specifically for Danny, made it harder for Karl to condition himself to accept that his brother was dead. Having a chance to say goodbye to Danny's dead face would have made it easier for him to accept Danny's death.

Karl was getting married to Sue-Anne Coaltonstone on New Year's Day, which would be a Wednesday. Karl never expected Danny would be killed on the front line so soon. Actually Karl was still getting over the shock that Sue-Anne even asked him to marry her. He just assumed Danny was going to be the lucky man.

Karl climbed down the ladder from his bed, for what felt like the millionth time, and forced himself to sit in front of his computer, Karl found General Ono's words more oppressive than he had ever felt them to be, before.

Karl was feeling an emptiness he never felt before. The twin he had lived with all his life was gone and no longer existed.

Karl did not believe in this war, he didn't know what side he was supposed to be on, or how General Ono could be an enemy force only a generation ago, and was now a liberator, which everyone in Unity was expected to fight for, not against. And he found it even harder to believe in the Transformation than to believe in this strange war.

He didn't even know if General Ono was a man or a robot.

Karl sat alone, and wished that he could be sharing this experience with friends and family; people who had cared about Danny. It was forbidden to waste time on such sentimentalities, when the nation was at war and in debt to the occupier regardless that it was Christmas Eve.

ESCAPE FROM TUT ISLAND

The draft had been in force for some time. On their eighteenth birthday it was required for the twins to enlist in the District 2021 division of the army.

The army accepted Danny and rejected Karl. Karl failed the aptitude test on purpose and starved himself so he would be too underweight for the army. Karl's plan partly backfired since his name had been assigned to the D list, which was a holding list for the Federation of Unity's Regiment of Botmen. In Karl's mind to become a botman was much more dehumanizing than being drafted into army life.

A simple doctor's note stating that Karl was fit enough to fight could transfer Karl's name from the D list to the A list at a moment's notice. The possibility of being turned into a botman hung over Karl's destiny like a black cloud. Dying in battle was one thing, but losing one's humanity while still living was a fate much worse, in Karl's opinion.

Their friends always said they both looked exactly alike on the outside and seemed to be the opposite on the inside.

Karl and Danny both loved moon gazing as much as they both loved Sue-Anne gazing.

When Karl saw the moon in the night sky, he could feel the heavenly powers looking down on him. It was hard to not believe in greater forces than General Ono's power on Earth when Karl gazed into the night sky. While life under the occupation stifled growth and thirst for adventure; the sky seemed to do the opposite. The sky went on forever without any known limits. Life under General Ono's occupation was a life consisting of one silly restriction after another.

From the time they were little boys, Danny and Karl dreamt of the day they would walk on their moon properties together.

The dream of going to the moon together was now shattered. Danny was dead. The shared dream, the only thing they both really had in common, besides their love for Sue-Anne, died before it had a chance to live. Just like Danny.

At the beginning, Sue-Anne was glued to Danny and loved him very much. For reasons unknown to Karl, shortly before Danny was called to the front line, Sue-Anne begged Karl to marry her.

As boys, most of their childhood nights were spent fighting over the telescope, until their parents had enough money to buy a second one. Danny would always win the shoving match that one night actually led to Karl falling from the rooftop.

As Karl fell, he felt the moonlight surround him; it felt magnetic and powerful.

Karl had sworn this power had somehow weakened the gravity around him and pulled him upward to soften his fall. Karl had no other explanation to why such a long fall did not kill him.

Karl vowed to himself, as he lay on the ground after the fall, that one day he would go to the moon. He would find that special power, and bring it back to Earth. Then the people would have their own special power to defend themselves from General Ono, or anyone who would destroy another man's right to be free.

Karl always wondered if such power could be owned, or if it was something that actually was given to a chosen few. Could one learn the process? Nevertheless, Karl thought that if there was a scientific explanation for this power then the process could be duplicated, once the formula was written.

Once Karl experienced floating he wanted to do it again. Danny was the only one he ever told his story to. They agreed that one day they would spend their vacation time on the moon, just so they could float.

ESCAPE FROM TUT ISLAND

Karl had work to do and needed to put the way he wished the world would be, out of his mind.

CHAPTER 4:
THE CITIZEN

Even though thousands of fighters were being killed in battle, for the Supreme Authority in the greater scheme of things, Tuesday afternoons in Pitville were pretty boring. Since it was Christmas Eve, Karl was feeling more let down than usual. He was also feeling a huge hole in his life, now that his brother was dead.

Karl couldn't imagine what it would be like to be blown up into little pieces in the heat of battle. He grossed himself out just thinking about his brother's guts being spread out all over the battlefield. Despite knowing that Danny could be killed in battle, Karl wasn't prepared for the feelings of hate he was beginning to feel for his own side.

Karl had little doubt Danny's ending was horrible. He was less certain Danny was living a new life on the other side.

Scientists were no longer able to work on projects that weren't directly beneficial to the war effort. Such projects included developing ways to reverse the algorithm of constant decay.

"What could have been, they will never know," Karl thought to himself.

As Karl stared at Danny's Certificate of Transformation and watched the Golden Seal change color for the millionth time, he wanted to believe life could be better as General Ono's Manifesto of Truth went on and on, the obstacles to a better life seemed impossible to overcome.

"Since your liberation, and as your Supreme Keeper of the Golden Scales, I am depending on you to help me maintain our balance. Balance gives our foundation equilibrium. Debtors must pay what they owe to Unity. The strength of Unity depends on this balance. Bills must be paid. We liberated you from extreme capitalism, liberation is a process," General Ono droned on.

"And liberation by an occupier is not freedom, it is imprisonment", Karl thought to himself.

"We must work every day to build peace and a quality of life worth living. While liberating you, we destroyed Tyranny and gave you unity. Without Unity you would be nothing more than beasts of burden. It is our unity that freed you and made you who you are today. The Federation of Unity will inspire you to fight for the real liberators, even though others on the mainland call us occupiers.

The Federation of Unity will grow stronger every day until death do us part. Together we are strong. Our fight for glory can never end. Happy Holidays everyone!" General Ono stopped shouting and lowered his voice as he lowered his fist. The reading of the morning's Manifesto of Truth was now complete.

CHAPTER 5:
RECYCLING DAY

Karl was grateful that the new year of 2076 would be starting next Wednesday, his wedding day.

Karl had spent most of December preparing to end and open new yearly accounts for his solvent clients. For his almost insolvent clients, he had just left their files in a pile on the left side of his desk.

The year of 2075 had been a brutal one.

He sighed as he tackled the pile of files which sat on the right corner of his desk. He deliberately avoided the pile on the left corner of his desk.

Karl felt drained. The stack of files on the left corner of his desk was growing out of control. Unknown to his clients, their bills were being paid through Karl's creativity. There were so many clients needing his help, he doubted that his creativity was powerful enough to help them al; still Karl tried.

Without Karl's help, those clients would have been insolvent months, if not years ago. General Ono said, in one of his readings from the Manifesto of Truth, that the new tax would make life easier for the common man. Karl knew better.

Once his poor clients became insolvent, who they used to be would no longer exist. Their family and friends would shun them. Once their clothes turned to rags, strangers would shun them too.

New ideas and work opportunities usually grew from another project's surplus, and progress depended on this surplus for its very existence. Without surplus coming from somewhere not much could change or grow. New ideas might start growing from the abyss, but material support would be needed if projects were to grow and live up to their true potential. Karl was now living in a time where life support for debtors was ceasing to exist.

What was the point of an idea if it could not become a new adventure, a new beginning, a new path?

The various schemes Karl created would be used to buy time for Karl's poorest clients. Could his actions be less moral, than no action, allowing his poverty-stricken clients to become insolvent and homeless, street people? These people would have been rounded up to be recycled, tonight, if it hadn't been for Karl's schemes. What a horrible thing to let happen to one's fellow man, on Christmas Eve.

Even though ideas could not bleed, they still died if not enacted; if the idea of goodwill toward man died, what then?

Karl was risking his life to protect the rights of his fellow man. He knew it was the right thing to do.

The only way Karl was able to save these people was by balancing their accounts with other people's money. And this balance was a thin line, indeed.

Karl's schemes to keep his clients solvent, temporarily, were now so interconnected that they would all collapse at once, if too many of his clients asked for their money back at the same time.

Most of Karl's clients were not aware that the order of things had already been preprogrammed. The Federation of Unity's Central Bank of Mina earned more profits whenever the cost of borrowing money increased. As the order of things became more rigid, the odds against survival became less certain.

"Why should these clients be made to become insolvent when there was plenty of money to go around if it wasn't being burnt as cannon fodder? Karl's clients had skills, and were nice people. Why should he write these people off as if these people meant less than the things in their house?" Karl wondered to himself.

There were so many people in similar situations as the clients whose files had been piling up on the left corner of Karl's desk. Karl sometimes wondered if he should just let them all die and knew that he couldn't; for it would be going against the rights of man and everything that he believed in.

Karl had been wishing for a better plan. He needed a system which would not collapse the way one source of cash flow was prone to do. But no other plan had ever come to mind.

"How could it be, the things that people once owned, were now being treated with more value than the people who once owned those things?" Karl had no idea how he could, in good conscience, look away while his fellow man's fate was being sealed by heartless occupiers.

Even though Karl only had the power to fix inequality between man and occupier temporarily, he believed that protecting the rights of man was his life's calling. How could he just stand by while people were being thrown away and recycled as casually as when people used to recycle their things?

As far as Karl could see, it was all about numbers. Anyone, including himself, would be doomed if more money went out than came in. And best practice was always about people, the numbers would come in later, sadly sometimes too late.

An unbearable sadness overpowered Karl. He wished the recycling and all the fighting would stop.

He thought he could hear the singing of Silent Night in the distance. He didn't know anyone personally who knew the words to that song; accept a few old timers.

ESCAPE FROM TUT ISLAND

From time to time Karl would forget how promising his own future was, when he immersed himself too deeply into his clients' troubles.

If given half a chance, Karl would have torn General Ono's mask from his face.

CHAPTER 6:
THE RIGHTS OF MAN
IN THE NEW ORDER OF THINGS

It was Wednesday morning. Karl lay awake all night staring at a lone spider as it made a web in the corner of his room. It did not feel anything like Christmas Day.

The siren blared.

Karl put on his glasses and then climbed down from his loft. He opened the curtains so he could see the street. It was cleaner than usual.

He sat on the hard chair and stared into the terminal. He only half listened to General Ono's speech which was being spoken in a halting fashion, emphasizing his arrogance and cruelty.

"Please join me this morning in thanking our Downtown Improvement Committees for making last night's recycling so successful. Tens of thousands of debtors were rounded up and will soon be given the chance to repay their debts. Now there will be less people to trespass against us; less people to contribute to the earth's tilting.

Debtors must pay back their debt to society.

At this very moment as I speak, tens of thousands of debtors and enemy fighters are being prepared to repay their debts to society and repay for the trespasses they made against us."

Karl reached for his com-corder phone, but it was not in his pocket. He remembered taking it out of his pocket and putting it on the dashboard of his car, last night. Karl hoped the phone was still there.

After listening to the reading from the Manifesto of Truth, Karl ran out into the rain so that he could determine if he had left his com-corder phone in his car. Karl was thankful to find his phone, even though the phoned seemed too hot for such a rainy miserable day.

Karl didn't think too long about it, since the rain was soaking him to his skin. He ran into his home and sat at his desk. He was about to phone his mother before he realized that the Roundup had been accidently recorded on his com-corder phone.

Botmen were marching in the thousands, many wearing black military uniforms and stomping their feet while swinging their batons menacingly in the rain. As Karl watched the Roundup on his com-corder phone, he realized how much he loathed the idea of being transformed into a botman.

Karl knew the routine by sound, but not by sight. The sound of feet stomping stopped. The destitute would be dragged away from their cardboard boxes hog-tied and forced into waiting trailer trucks.

There was little gentleness shown as young mothers were separated from their children. There were so many people being rounded up, Karl wondered if rumors were true, that General Ono was only partially human and mostly robotic. Why would a man like that, care about the rights of man? How could he?

Though he knew the numbers, he never tried to imagine what it would look like to see thousands of people actually being hog-tied and thrown into truck trailers. Black helicopters and botflies were hovering overhead. The botflies were being piloted from battle stations somewhere under the base in Coalton. Thousands of guards, some human and some hybrid, either stood in full view or were sitting inside black armed tanks.

Karl played the video over and over again. He watched as the homeless, now called street people, were taken away. Karl felt a deep sense of loss and wondered why. He had lost nothing personally. He did not recognize any of these people that were taken away to be recycled. These people were strangers. He did not know why he felt a bond with them.

As Karl watched the scene unfold, he saw a young woman running away from the botmen. And even though most were captured, this one woman was actually able to escape. He felt incredibly uplifted when he realized that this girl was actually escaping her preprogrammed fate.

One of the botmen appeared to have let her escape; either because he had too many people to chase or he wanted her to escape because he liked her.

Perhaps the girl's angelic face struck the guard as being too beautiful to be destroyed.

It was hard to know what actually motivated the botman. Karl knew he would have done the same.

Karl wondered how the future would turn out for the girl who escaped the Roundup. Did her beauty persuade the guard to let her go? Karl understood how such beauty could drive most men to forget about their own self-interest for a moment; in this case, possibly a fatal moment.

Now that this escapee had been pulled into the fight to protect her own humanity; she would have a chance to experience her natural strength and possibly grow to her full potential and maybe even join him in his quest to protect the rights of man.

CHAPTER 7:
THE DETAINER

Karl played the video again. He counted the botflies which were flying above the girl's head while she was escaping. Feelings stirred in him that he had never felt for anyone else before, not even Sue-Anne. This girl could have been his twin soul during gentler times.

As Karl watched the video of the Roundup he wished that he could do something to help. He never realized people actually escaped during the Roundup. The idea made him a little more hopeful concerning his own future.

The sudden knocking on the door jolted Karl out of his daydream. He hid his com-corder phone as fast as he could.

Trying to be brave, Karl opened the door and to his surprise he actually knew the official at the door. It was Mrs. Elizabeth Stern wearing a Santa hat and holding her pet Chihuahua, Teacup. A flying gun was hovering by her side. Mrs. Stern was employed by so many ministries, no one was certain which ministry was her primary employer. It was said that the Ministry of Vagrancy and a classified committee overseen by the Ministry of Justice, were her main employers, but no one knew for sure. She was also president for the two Downtown Improvement Committees, for both Pitville and Coalton. This was the position she would use to introduce herself to Karl.

Mrs. Stern, put Teacup on the floor and proceeded to show Karl her identification. He glanced at the seal to verify that the Golden Scales changed color. Karl nodded politely being careful to show deference to Mrs. Stern's authority. The Flying Spying Gun hovering by Mrs. Stern's side was so distracting that Karl didn't even notice that Teacup had just peed on his shoe.

"Kneel, Karl."

"Karl knelt obediently before her.

When asked his name, he replied with a stutter that always appeared when he was frightened.

He tried to remain calm, as he sputtered out; "KKKarl PPParks, Ma'am," while avoiding Mrs. Stern's eyes.

Mrs. Stern continued speaking in her usual harsh and condescending tone. She explained that Karl was under investigating, even though this point was self-evident.

Mrs. Stern explained that the investigation was due to a complaint Karl's computer, Delta-C made in regards to his breaking rule number 2021during the reading from the Manifesto of Truth, on Monday morning and then trying to tamper with its database possibly to destroy evidence of the deed.

"What do you plead, guilty or innocent?" Mrs. Stern demanded to know.

"I am neither."

"That plea of 'neither', if it is a plea, is not an option, Karl. People like you need to know your place and respect authority since we know what is best for you. Why did you leave your post?" Mrs. Stern demanded to know. She waved her electronic documentation in Karl's face, missing Karl's nose, only by chance.

"I just received a letter that my brother, my twin brother, passed on in battle, MMMonday," Karl said as he kept his head bowed.

"You must be very proud. Always remember that pride cometh before a fall. So never be too proud," Mrs. Stern said as she made a note on her laptop.

"Yes Ma'am."

"You are a very lucky young man. Your brother has made you a primary relative of a holder of the Green Badge for Military Merit," Mrs. Stern said in her usual condescending tone, as she picked up Teacup. Karl wasn't sure what to say or what to do next.

"Bad thoughts live in people's minds sometimes forever. You young people must learn before you are able to overcome them," Mrs. Stern warned as Karl wondered what if any idea, good or bad, had the same chance to succeed without having an influence on social reality. Karl supposed that bad ideas would have more hope to succeed. People just expected bad outcomes these days; good outcomes on the other hand needed convincing to be believable. And why did so many good ideas have to be written down before they are forgotten while bad ideas are so hard to forget? Karl did not know.

"An important announcement was scheduled on Monday and you not only broke the law by leaving your post that day; you could have been left out of the loop designated for your District's collective consciousness. You are required to pay close attention to every detail when General Ono is reading the Manifesto of Truth. You must remember that all objects when set in motion stay in motion along the same path, so don't be a fool and lose sight of the path towards winning."

Karl wanted to yell out that he was not an object and had a spirit of a free man, and was born to inherit the noble cause to protect the rights of man, even if it meant his own death, when doing so.

"What was the reason for leaving your post, Karl? Missing your brother is no excuse. We all miss our relatives who have died in war; nevertheless we all find the time to read personal mail after General Ono's readings.

"I was having explosive diarrhea," Karl said meekly, knowing that the grief if held in, could over time, burn a hole in his stomach lining.

"I tampered with the logs to save myself from the embarrassment of explaining my predicament," Karl hoped this story would help him avoid being detained for further questioning. Last thing he wanted to do was miss his Christmas lunch with Sue-Anne.

"Mrs. Stern stopped waving the document in front of his face

Karl kept his head bowed. Suddenly his stomach ejaculated an acid type fluid. He swallowed it and coughed uncontrollably. Mrs. Stern stepped back, hoping to avoid whatever germs that were sputtering from Karl's face.

Mrs. Stern handed him the stylus while trying to avoid getting too close to Karl's germs.

"Use this to sign that," she ordered. As Karl reached for the stylus, which was a difficult task to undertake, since he was still kneeling and Mrs. Stern was very tall; his stomach ejaculated even more acid, making him cough all over the Mrs. Stern's electronic pad. Karl signed the document anyway.

"I am so very sorry, Ma'am."

Mrs. Stern glared at Karl. The look on her face revealed Mrs. Stern's deep fear of germs giving Karl a fleeting moment of control. The moment did not last long. Mrs. Stern's Flying Spying Gun changed position so it could hover above Karl's head.

Without letting go of her eye contact with Karl, Mrs. Stern wiped the fluid from the electronic pad before she verified that the document had been signed correctly. Karl turned his eyes inward, and continued to bow his head.

"You may rise," Mrs. Stern said as she typed a new note into her electronic pad. She scanned Karl's forehead one more time to verify that the note she had just written was included in the database which was allocated to Karl's life-long database.

"Remember, Karl, in order to be part of Unity, which is not just a privilege, but a state of mind, you must focus on Unity, not just yourself. You must master your mind or we will do it for you.

I almost forgot, we have another complaint about you, related to your behavior downtown. You know I have a very important position on the two Downtown Improvement Committees, anyway, I have been told that you shop in the Pitville Grocery Store for small quantity items when we all know you should be shopping for small quantity items in the Pitville Convenience Store. It is troubling for those busy clerks in the only grocery store downtown, to serve you, when you buy in such small quantities. It just isn't worth their time."

"I understand," Karl lied.

"As the president of the two Downtown Improvement committees I am aware of how our social programming is complaint driven. A few years back, there was fear that the good people of Coalton were going to lose their library to those unsavory homeless people who wander around downtown in such a pitiful state in front of the children. The militias were called and after a few sessions of brainstorming we came up with the recycling program, which, as we all know, is second to none. You see Karl what is good often comes from something bad and burdensome. What did you just say Karl?"

"I didn't say anything, Mrs. Stern."

"No Karl, you did say something, it sounded like you swore at me. Do you know what we do, in Coalton Valley to unsavory characters?

"Mrs. Stern you know I wouldn't swear at you or anyone and I have lived here all my life."

"Karl, I am talking about the new Coalton Valley. I must include this unpleasant incident in my report."

"Thank you for your cooperation and Merry Christmas. Oh one more thing Karl, you must remember that you are not entitled to any expectations. You people were fooled by your expectations before your liberation. You people never questioned how mathematically impossible it was for a good man to win an election. You people never did anything about the incompetents who were running for public office just to split the vote so that the moneyed men could win. And another thing Karl, the voice in your mind is a beast. Only General Ono has the power to humanize people like you," Mrs. Stern said as she picked up Teacup and checked her shoes; making sure that they were still shiny before she walked out of the door.

Without any goodbye Mrs. Stern left the house as quickly as she could, hoping to avoid catching any germs Karl might be carrying.

Karl felt completely demoralized after being detained by Mrs. Stern. He quickly cleaned up after Teacup then returned to his post at his computer terminal.

The mid-morning reading was playing in the background. The reading was so boring Karl's craving for coffee became uncontrollable. Coffee made him feel more alive. Well at least more alive than Danny was right now.

"The Power of Unity flows through each one of us. We must never remove the chips that link us as one. We must stay linked. We must continue as one for the sake of Unity."

Karl hated his chips. He hated the invasion of privacy that the chips in his body imposed. And without privacy a man was afraid to be his genuine self.

"We shun all failures and people who fail to pay their debts. Our lives must reflect balance for the Golden Scales will be testing us, every day. We must trust that the Golden Scales will grant us balance," General Ono said as the drums kept time to his drawling speech.

ESCAPE FROM TUT ISLAND

Karl was too wound up to concentrate on work. He was thinking about the Flying Spying Gun, and wondered about its technology. He was also thinking about the girl who escaped the Roundup and wondered where she was at this very moment and whether she was cold, hungry or frightened.

Karl wondered if someone could just grab a Flying Spying Gun when the owner wasn't looking, and just reprogram it. Could anyone just decide someone should be shot, and program facial recognition commands into the gun, and no one would know who it was who had ordered another to be murdered?

Guns, the way Karl knew them to be, usually had a person at the other end doing the shooting. Imagine if governments and rivals could shoot amongst themselves while never knowing who their opponent really was.

It was Christmas day and Karl didn't feel very Christmassy. He wished for a world filled with goodwill instead of the one he was being forced to live in.

CHAPTER 8:
THE LIQUIDATORS

Karl was now free to resume his usual duties so he poured himself another cup of coffee. There was something he was supposed to do but he couldn't remember what it was because he was so traumatized by Mrs. Stern's visit. He checked his spam mail from various underground liquidators who brokered in the trade of misery. The property, once owned by the dispossessed, was now fought over by the most ruthless liquidators in the industry. Often these liquidators offered Karl bribes if he revealed insider information related to whose property would be up next for grabs.

The Federation of Unity's Central Bank of Mina had many employees who did elect to sell out personal information to these brokers which traded in the property and body parts of the dispossessed. The misery being caused through these transactions mattered to no one, especially not to the liquidators and the Old Boys Club.

These people mattered to Karl; for they were his clients.

He rubbed his identification chip in his hand absentmindedly. His hand tingled the way it often did when his chip was either being updated or for a reason which was unknown to him.

Most of the time, he didn't really think about the ID chips, which had been in his body since birth. One chip was in his hand and the other was in his forehead. These chips were facts of his life that were out of his control.

ESCAPE FROM TUT ISLAND

To become chipless was to become dispossessed. Karl's identification proved that he was a citizen therefore he was still able to enjoy his rights as a documented man. The chips were always in his body, and he had a faint scar and random tingling to prove it. The chips were linked to the Ministry of Social Security. An identity file was opened the day Karl was born and would be closed the day he died. He supposed that Danny's file was now closed.

The original purpose of the I.D. chips was to trace children when they went missing. During the early zeros, child abduction was very common. If a child had the misfortune of being abducted, he might not ever find out who he used to be, or where he came from. The technology was so successful in identifying abducted children; the project was expanded to include all newborn babies.

The ID chips linked all citizens in the Federation to a centralized database. Without valid identification a person was prohibited from buying or selling goods and services only because they were not given any other way to buy access to those goods and services. Karl hated this near cashless society, and still had a small stash of cash hidden under his bed, in case the local banks failed again.

As Karl stared at his reflection, self-doubt began to take over his mind. He was certain Danny never felt the kind of doubt about himself that he was feeling today. He wanted to plan the part of his future he was able to plan, as wisely as he could, but he knew that there were so many factors out of his control, which could take over his life without a moment's notice. He wanted to be successful. He wanted Sue-Anne to be proud of him.

Thoughts of Sue-Anne jolted Karl's memory into realizing that it was almost noon and he was supposed to be meeting her for Christmas lunch. The Christmas present he intended to give Sue-Anne was still unwrapped. He fumbled in his underwear drawer and found the long rectangular box. He opened it and admired the gold necklace for a second or two. After wrapping the gift as best as he good; he found a bow in his sock drawer and positioned it in the middle of the box. Karl placed the gift in his pocket beside his com-corder phone.

He was annoyed with himself that he allowed himself to be so distracted. While trying to hurry, Karl cut his face shaving. He swore quietly to himself, and decided that he would break down and spend money on new razor blades after lunch. He combed his hair and struggled with a tangle, and pulled out a clump of hair, realizing for the first time that he might be going bald.

He pulled out a clean white suit and proceeded to dress. He tried to focus his thoughts on Sue-Anne but all he could think about was the woman who was able to escape the Roundup. He couldn't stop himself from wondering how she was holding up.

It had stopped raining. Karl decided to walk to the café.

CHAPTER 9:
THE GATHERING

Joan wasn't able to sleep much. Last night was the worst Christmas Eve that she had ever known. She woke up several times to the pitch dark, cold air, feeling so lost it terrified her. She was sure that her fear was contributing to her splitting headache. The hunger gnawing at her stomach kept her awake. She was finding it harder to think as her hunger grew stronger. If it hadn't been for her hunger the loss of her mother would have been dominating her mind.

Her clothes were soaking wet and she was afraid that she would freeze to death. She felt guilty for escaping last night's Roundup for recycling, and didn't know why. She had no idea how she was going to continue to live. She did not want to die in hiding; watching helplessly as her life faded away. She wanted to fight back the way her grandfather would have wanted her to do, just for the sake of human dignity, if nothing else.

Surviving as a debtor under General Ono's occupation was not something Joan was prepared for. She never expected this to happen to her. She had always been wary of taking on too many student loans. Nevertheless she was determined not to become pitiful and helpless, even though she owed over one hundred thousand dollars in student loans to the occupiers; she wanted to believe in the future. She wanted to believe in love. One day she wanted to have children.

Life, as Joan knew it to be, was filled with sad events. She often called the path she was following, the

Goodwin curse, which made her name sound like a cruel joke. Her father used to always joke that they were the Bad-loss family not the Goodwins.

Joan's father died suddenly of a heart attack in his sleep. For one year Joan and her mother struggled to make ends meet. Finally, when there was no more money that could be borrowed nor found, and the debts continued to grow, the black file arrived. Joan's mother refused to steal money and she would not allow Joan to steal either.

The enforcers were soon knocking on the Goodwins' door and forced them out of their home. Then the locks were changed and they were forbidden to return. The change in Goodwins' citizenship status was documented in the Detachment's database, and a mark on their forehead and hand were all that were left when their identity chips were removed. Their creditors owned everything they thought was theirs.

At first, Joan and her mother were allowed to stay in shelters, but soon their time ran out and they were forced to live on the streets.

Joan had no idea what gave her the energy which pulled her to safety. Once she started to run, she just kept running, with Snowy setting the pace. It was very doubtful that her mother survived.

In the back of her mind, Joan always had a vague plan that she would try to hide in the tunnels that were used to access and transport coal during the Coal Wars; decades before General Ono's occupation. Those were the days when the Minese miners were being used as undocumented worker-slaves during illegal mining operations. Joan's grandfather, Ginger Goodwin, sketched out maps of the tunnels he was familiar with, during the days following the Pitville Mine disaster, when he was trapped in Mine Five. Joan still had the sketches though she did not know why her attraction to them was so strong, she could not let go of them. Joan said a silent prayer to the grandfather she never knew, thankful that his maps had given her the idea to find this place and the ability to find an unsealed opening to the old tunnels. She was cold and hungry and she didn't know when she would become dangerously close to getting hypothermia; nevertheless, she felt a faint sense of peace, without knowing why. Nothing made any sense.

Longing to share her life with other people, she hoped that she was not the only one who was able to escape. She cringed when she thought how awful it must be for her mother. She could not bare to imagine her mother being torn apart, limb by limb.

She wasn't sure if she should be thankful that she was hearing human voices or whether she should be very afraid. Joan could hear people talking nearby and wondered if they were the ones who were singing Silent Night, last night. She wondered if the people nearby were in the same situation. Joan had experienced enough grief for a lifetime and didn't think that she could bare any more pain. She hoped if there were others nearby that they would be on her side.

Joan didn't think that she could survive on her own. And even if she could, she didn't want to live the rest of her life alone, as an outcast.

It felt like the whole world was either against her or had forgotten her. She wondered if the people nearby would be friendly or hostile. She hoped that they would be strong people and hadn't already gone mad. Joan could hear the faint voices again and she hoped these voices were coming from good people or at least not enemies. She lay on the damp ground holding Snowy. She tried to think of thoughts which could comfort her.

If only the botmen would stay away from these tunnels; maybe she could stay alive for a little while longer.

If life was still the survival of the fittest, Joan wondered how long she could survive like this. She did not feel very fit. She was cold, dirty and hungry and her head was hurting in a way she had never experienced before. At nineteen years old, she felt like an old woman.

Deciding that finding food should be her main concern, Joan picked herself up from the wet ground. Her pain was overwhelming her but she persevered. She knew she had to find food even if it meant begging for it. She hated walking in public looking so ragged and broken. She hated the way people turned away from her as she begged for food and sometimes even laughed. She hated the thought of leaving the tunnel. She felt safe in this tunnel.

Despite these inhumane conditions she was being forced to live in, Joan still wanted to live. Though she hated her life the way it was now, it wasn't really life which she hated and she decided to make a conscious effort to cling to the little hope she could muster up, since after all, it was Christmas Day.

Wanting to live long enough to avenge the wrongs General Ono and the occupiers had committed against her mother, she also wanted to live her life as a good person; a woman of whom her mother would be proud.

Sleep weaved Joan's thoughts into a vivid dream. She dreamt that she was leading a huge army of creatures with ape bodies and human heads. Most of her army had Stun Guns to carry and a flock of giant eagles were leading the way. In her dream she was walking holding hands with a frail young man as they tip toed through a field of dying people. She could see another man, who looked identical to the one she was walking with, riding a horse, which changed from shades of white to shades of black as he rode towards her. By the time the young man was standing by her side, his horse was black.

Joan woke up to the familiar hunger pains gnawing at her stomach forcing her to think about searching for food. After having such a strange dream, she felt renewed and even more determined to stay alive. She vowed that she would stay alive, no matter what. She vowed to overcome any obstacle in her path. She would defy General Ono and would refuse to let fear and hopelessness take over her mind or her sense of direction.

A faint smell of food was lingering in the air. It had been three days that she was homeless and destitute and she had to eat something in order to stay alive. Like the animal she felt she was becoming, she let her instincts overcome her fears as she crawled through the muddy damp tunnel following the scent hoping to find something, anything to eat.

Joan followed the scent and found herself inside an abandoned room, or more accurately an intersection where many tunnels came together. Two young men and one young woman most likely in their late teens were sitting around a pot of soup which was cooking over a small fire. The borehole above channeled the smoke upward.

"Who are you?" The woman demanded to know.

"My name is Joan Goodwin," Joan said wondering if these two young men who looked nearly identical were somehow part of her dream.

"On second thought, I don't care who you are, go away."

Wishing to not grow weaker than she already was, Joan decided to explain her situation to the entire group.

"I haven't eaten in three days, I need help."

"Why don't you eat your dog," Ashley Coaltonstone snarled as she reached out to Snowy, startling him. Snowy growled and showed his teeth, and then lay back down and closed his eyes.

"Your dog tried to bite me," Ashley whimpered, as she moved away from Snowy.

Jason Bell sat back and tried to think of something to say that could break the ice.

"Your dog sure has great teeth; they will probably last longer than ours," Jason said as Justin shook his head disapprovingly.

"Snowy and I are too weak to bite anyone," Joan Goodwin responded while trying to remain calm. "I have no idea what I am going to do now. I escaped the cleansing. And I am not sure if that is a good thing."

"We are eating this Christmas Day soup and trying to create a feeling of goodwill," Justin said half in jest and half seriously.

"We are actually hoping to reach the Arctic District while we are still young. I hear that they pay in cash and that there is a lot of mining and laundry work up there. Maybe we could still have careers, raise a family and have a life. We are imagining what we could be, in another district, if we could leave this behind us," Jason explained, as he lay down closing his eyes.

"I feel awful," Joan admitted.

"Well you look awful too," Ashley said as she kept her distance from Snowy.

"We guys are at our best when we are protecting women," Justin Bell said as he patted Snowy on the head. Snowy raised his head and licked Justin's hand encouraging Joan to trust him. Snowy always seemed to be a good judge of character.

Not wanting to be upstaged by Justin, Jason agreed saying; "Man's spirit can soar to greatness when called upon to defend a beautiful woman."

Ashley scoffed and rolled her eyes.

"I am glad you found us," Jason said as he shook Joan Goodwin's hand.

"I am Jason Bell and Justin is my brother. We have been hiding here for about six months," Jason said.

"I knew you two were related," Joan said as laughter broke out and echoed along the walls of the dismal tunnel.

"That is a good one. We have been here ever since the anti-vagrancy law began. We never stop being afraid. The sooner we get to the Arctic the better off we will be!"

Jason Bell exclaimed as his twin brother nodded in agreement.

"As long as we remain in this zone, we will always be hungry and angry. We will never get our old lives back, but we can't forget who we used to be, before our lives were taken from us," Justin added.

"You have to join us," Jason said before Ashley could protest.

"No one can survive alone. We need each other. We need to fight for each other's wellbeing, even when fighting for ourselves feels hopeless, if we have others to fight for and protect, we will only grow stronger. Isn't that right Ashley?" Jason said realizing that the dirt on Joan's face made her look stunning, possibly because it contrasted with her angelic face.

"I think we should eat her dog. It would be the best meal we have had for months," Ashley said as she helped herself to another bowl of soup.

Snowy began to whimper as he moved closer to Joan.

"Ashley, don't forget our plan. We are going to get out of this district and head north. We will need a dog to maintain our pace, possibly to help us hunt. And he is the perfect color. Once we get out of this district, everything will be different," Justin said, as he glared in Ashley's direction. His teeth chattered with cold.

Joan would have given anything to be in another place in time with this young man, perhaps sharing a meal, listening to music and laughing together.

"I don't know how I escaped. Snowy started to run, and I followed. I felt that I was being pulled towards this tunnel and I thought that I could hear someone singing Silent Night, last night," Joan said feeling ashamed of her appearance. Her dirty white suit was torn and shabby looking. Everyone in the group looked just as shabby as

Joan. She realized that pride had more to do with falling than surviving.

"If it weren't for Snowy, I don't think I would have even thought of running away. I felt so beaten down. Snowy kept running, and I followed. I owe him my life."

"Hooray for Snowy," Justin replied as he retrieved a bottle of water from his pack, opened it and held it for Snowy to drink. We would never eat your dog," Jason promised. "We are fighting for our dignity not just our lives. We still live by the code of conduct which separates men of merit from thugs."

"It is true," Ashley said. "We have survived even when our so called friends and family turned their backs on us. I am related to the Coaltonstones and I wouldn't go back now, even if they begged me to come back."

"Well, at least most of your family is still alive. I suppose that is what happens when you sell your soul to the winning party. We need resources to back up our plan. If we ever leave this hellhole district we will need a miracle," Jason concluded.

"I suppose goodwill was the structuring of the Christmas miracle, the last hope of the doomed," Justin interjected.

"Everyone we knew turned their backs on us. Our parents were captured. I looked back and saw them being hogtied. It was terrible," Jason said as he stretched his long legs.

"Same with me, I just kept running. I looked back once or twice. I saw my mother being hogtied. Snowy just kept running, and I ran as fast as I could to keep up with him."

There would have been a time when Joan would have noticed everyone's tattered shoes. Now, the things she used to take for granted didn't matter so much. It was easier that way than to miss everything she had in her old life. All shoes wear out, sooner or later, regardless if they are kept under your bed or are still on your feet as you sleep. It was ridiculous to be judging this boy or anyone for the condition of their shoes in times like these, especially when her suit was just as dirty and tattered as everyone else's.

Joan wished that she and Justin could find a way to be frozen in time so they could avoid the effect these rough conditions would soon have on their health and appearance.

"I looked back, so I did see my mother getting hog tied too. I wished with all my heart that I could find a way to help her and myself. It was horrible. Snowy kept running, and I kept running. I knew of this place sort of. I think this place is on my grandfather's map that he made a long time ago. I also felt like I was being pulled into this place if you know what I mean."

"We don't need another mouth to feed," Ashley complained.

Without waiting for Joan's reply and without further argument, Jason gave Joan a bowl of very thin soup and a piece of bread to go with it.

Joan didn't blame Ashley for being so unfriendly, but she was truly afraid that if Ashley were hungry enough, she would eat Snowy. She knew they were only protecting what little they had. There were trying to be winners in a game they had already lost.

Jason poured the soup into a bowl and waited for it to cool before he gave it to Snowy. Snowy jumped to his feet when he realized that the soup was meant for him. The bowl moved around the floor with the force of each lap that Snowy took.

Jason gave Snowy a second bowl of soup. Ashley was outraged.

"What? You are giving that dog a second bowl of soup when we only get one bowl each? What are we going to do when we run out of soup? I suppose if we get hungry enough; it could feel right eating the dog or even each other," Ashley said before storming out of the clearing and vanishing into one of the tunnel and out of sight.

"Ashley doesn't mean any harm. Don't worry about her, she is really scared. Things were done to her that she won't talk about. Too many bad vibes sooner or later will change a person," Justin explained as he tried to reassure Joan that Ashley didn't really eat dogs or other human beings; not yet anyway.

Joan sat on the damp ground beside Justin and sipped her hot soup slowly.

"Well how do we know what we will turn into if we live like this for too long? I wish there was somewhere that we could go and were welcomed; a place where we could live like human beings again."

"We all do. We are hoping to go somewhere where we will belong. Like we said before, our plan is the Arctic. We don't want to feel as if we are just leaving somewhere and going nowhere. We want to find a place where we too can feel human again. Ashley wants that too. She will come around," Jason added.

"Thank you for your kindness. Believe it or not, this is turning out to be not too bad of a Christmas after all."

"You are the one that is brightening up our day, Joan. It is hard to not be angry, so much has been taken away from us," Justin said as he watched Joan and his brother eat their soup.

Despite Jason's reassurance, Joan felt uneasy around Ashley. Joan felt that she was being watched whenever Ashley was nearby. Ashley gave her the creeps. Joan tried not to look too anxious as she ate her soup.

"I wonder when the botflies are going to surround this place," Joan asked realizing that she should have worded her question a little less harshly. Joan was terrified of the botflies.

"No one knows, we have to stay positive or the uncertainty will certainly drive us mad." Jason pondered on his own words as he fed Snowy a piece of his own bread.

"We have been expecting them for months. But the botflies and botguards seem to either not know that we are here, or they are leaving us alone," Jason tried not to sound terrified of the botflies. Everyone agreed to put the enemy out of their minds so they could enjoy the little soup they had. They needed to conserve their energy, for the path they were about to share would be a long one.

"I have these maps my granddaddy, Ginger Goodwin made when he was trapped in Mine Five during the great Pitville Mine Disaster of 2030. This is all I have left from that side of the family. I suppose this is all I have left, period."

"So Ginger Goodwin was your granddaddy? I remember that story. Our granddaddy used to tell us all kinds of stories about your granddaddy. One thing about your granddaddy; he knew when to take a stand and he knew when to pull away.'

Ashley returned from the darkness of the tunnels and sat close to Jason.

"What are you talking about? This is a man who was found dead, as maggots were eating his face," Ashley responded with indignity.

"Well that man was rumored to be your brother," Justin replied in Ginger Goodwin's defense.

"Shut up, you are being rude."

"Lighten up Ash. Technically how rude is it for a great aunt to look the same age as her great niece?" Justin interjected.

"Anyway those rumors were just rumors," Ashley said in her defense.

"It is his birthday today," Joan interjected.

"That is right; it is Ginger Goodwin's birthday today. I guess the story which is the most inspiring to us, is that Ginger Goodwin buried the proceeds from the settlement he made with old man, James Coaltonstone, after Christina, I suppose she was your grandmother, broke his heart," Justin said while deciding to not mention all the stories he heard about Ginger Goodwin dodging the draft.

"The treasure is supposed to be somewhere in these tunnels," Jason added.

"I never heard anything about it. Actually my mother refused to discuss Daddy's side of the family and so did Daddy, she said it would be rude to do so. I always remembered my Grandfather's birthday though, every Christmas Day."

"Don't you think it was mean to treat that side of the family like a dirty secret?" Justin asked, quickly changing the subject.

"Not really, everyone knew all there was to know."

"I suppose you heard about the time your grandfather almost ran out of air, trapped in Mine Five after he saved the whole morning crew from descending into the mine minutes before it exploded? Justin asked.

"Justin! Joan already explained the circumstances which led to her grandfather drawing all those maps he left her," Jason interjected.

"Well actually he left them to his descendants, he never met me and I never met him. My grandmother was carrying my father at the time," Joan explained

"The Pitville Mine Disaster happened just around this time, 45 years ago. I suppose those times weren't so great either," Justin noted.

"Maybe we should combine efforts. We have been down here since June," Justin added.

"How do you live?" Joan asked.

"We have been eating bats. These tunnels are full of them. And there are water pools here and there, after it rains. We stock up on water. It is a pretty awful existence, but we are still alive. We are getting to know our way around here. We could use the railway track they used to haul undocumented coal through to the Bering Strait, and escape Tut Island."

"You mean District 2021, Justin. This is no longer Tut Island. I still love Tut Island but I hate District 2021, it feels like a debtors' prison," Ashley interjected.

"Yes, because District 2021 in many ways is a debtors' prison. Joan, your grandfather's maps may give us a clue or two." Justin suggested.

"About what?"

"You must know that your grandfather is rumored to have buried his gold bullion down here?" Justin asked.

"Actually I heard rumors but I never believed them. While I was growing up, people told me stories once they knew Ginger Goodwin was my grandfather. But my dad and mom never talked about it. I know the story goes that my grandfather converted an undisclosed payment James Coaltonstone gave him from North American currency into gold bullion. I never knew what to believe about my grandfather," Joan explained.

"Now your brother has done it. If we find it, we will have to split it with a fourth person," Ashley whispered to Jason as she pulled him into a pitch black corner of a nearby tunnel. "What is wrong with your brother? Is he expecting us to split the gold with her if we find it? I mean I thought, besides hiding from the Backbencher Kids, we were trying to find the treasure Ginger Goodwin is said to have buried down here.

"We must not alienate her," Jason whispered back. "She may be holding the missing part of the puzzle. And besides technically she could be your great niece."

Joan felt uncomfortable since it was obvious Ashley and Jason were talking about her, but she understood the risk people were taking these days, whenever they trusted anyone.

"Ignore those two. My grandfather believed in your grandfather. He used to say Ginger Goodwin had a heart of gold, and was too good of a person to even consider playing the social games, therefore would have been too honest of a person to actually be Deep Coal," Justin said wishing his grandfather were still alive.

"Well my grandfather used to say the opposite. He used to say Ginger Goodwin had a heart as black as coal," Ashley interjected as she appeared from the shadows with Jason. Ashley did not bring up the fact her grandfather was not only rumored to be Ginger's father but her own father. If the rumors were true, Ginger would be her brother and technically she would be Joan's great aunt. Her legal father was Bobby Coaltonstone; Bobby Coaltonstone was the ventilation engineer in Mine Five and was found responsible for the Pitville Mining disaster of 2030 and was convicted of criminal negligence. He served a lengthy prison sentence with few conjugal visits.

"Under General Ono, family ties are just as artificial as drinking beer to simulate artificial joy. I still think you were snooping around so you could find the treasure and keep it for yourself."

"No. I don't know anything about a treasure. I took shelter here, partly due to my grandfather's map and partly because I had no idea what to do. I really want to find a way out of this nightmare without having to kill myself," Joan explained.

"Don't be scared of us Joan. You know what our grandfather used to say that your grandfather used to say all the time?"

"What?"

"You can't score a goal if you don't get out on the field!" Jason and Justin said in unison and then laughed hysterically.

"What is it about men, Joan? Every time something happens they manage to compare it to a sport. We are fighting for our lives and future and these guys are comparing it all to soccer.

"Well my grandfather played soccer at almost pro level, but he had problems with his lungs and of course he had been under suspicion for years that he was the one behind 'Deep Coal'.

"Yes, that part of the story was always so weird. How could your grandfather be a whistleblower at the same as he was trapped in the mine, cut off from civilization? At the time everyone thought he had been incinerated," Jason wondered out loud.

"Everyone but your Grandmother, Christina," Justin noted.

"All I remember is that my dad always said that nothing good would come out of the Black Diamonds' Curse for the negativity which it brings is overpowering," Joan replied.

It was nice to have hot soup but Joan was afraid of the danger this luxury may bring. She ignored her fears and ate her meager Christmas meal with the three strangers she hoped would become her friends. If all the rumors she heard were true about her own grandfather and great-grandfather, then technically Ashley Coaltonstone could actually be her great aunt and the only blood relative she had left.

S. E. MCKENZIE

CHAPTER 10:
RECYCLING DEPOT

It was just like any other busy Wednesday morning at the House of Detachment; where many Federation of Unity offices, including the Central Bank of Mina, were located.

Allan Bell sat at his desk, wishing that he could spend Christmas day with his wife and kids. Feeling overwhelmed by all the work he was scheduled to do, he closed his eyes and imagined a day when he could be free to do whatever he pleased.

The House of Detachment was home to thousands of government offices, but Allan's office was one of the most luxurious. His office was situated on the 84th floor and the skyline view was breathtaking.

Allan Bell worked for the Ministry of Transformation but his duties would often lead to internal contacts with other ministries whose offices were found on lower floors in the same building.

Today had been an unusually difficult day. Allan was in charge of processing 101,595 bodies. Many of these bodies had been captured last night either on the battlefield or during the roundup of the debtors. General Ono had no respect for the Christmas Holiday that was for sure. Allan loved Christmas Day. It was his favorite day of the year.

The Ministry of Transformation and the Ministry of Vagrancy were working closely with the Pitville and Coalton Downtown Improvement Committees and their sub group, the Justice Alliance, was overseen by the Ministry of Justice. Allan had no idea why he was working with the two Downtown Improvement Committees.

The two Downtown Improvement Committees were requesting that all the applicable records from the Ministry of Transformation and the Ministry of Vagrancy be sent to the Justice Alliance by tomorrow afternoon. Allan had a team of one hundred employees working on this project yet he still felt understaffed and wasn't sure why these documents were being sent to the Justice Alliance and not to the Ministry of Defense. Allan was not sure why the Downtown Improvement committees for Coalton and Pitville were involved in the issuing of orders related to this project at all.

This was the first time that Allan worked with the Justice Alliance, and found this request to be quite unusual. The change in protocol would appear to vindicate the spreading of the rumors that were growing rampant between the 76th and 84th floors. Allan had no idea why the Ministry of Transformation was working so closely with the Justice Alliance and the two Downtown Improvement Committees. The rumors he had been hearing, here and there, were now appearing to be more than just idle gossip.

Allan usually didn't question the recycling of debtors. He agreed with the program since the debtors did have arrears owing to the Federation of Unity's Central Bank of Mina. The recycling of these debtors did relieve the suffering of others who had sacrificed dearly to the Federation of Unity, during various battles over the years. Allan could see the improvement in morale as fighters from the front line were fitted with new organic limbs and internal organs. These fighters sacrificed for the greater good; therefore the cruelty of recycling human beings was justified.

Day by day, Allan was finding evidence that body parts were secretly being sold to wealthy oil sheiks and coal barons in foreign lands. This concerned him but he did not let his superiors know. He spoke as little as possible to the people that he worked with. He mostly just listened.

Though, Allan didn't want to believe it was true, there was no other reasonable explanation for the sudden increase in foreigners of high standing, visiting district 2021. Tut Island was no longer an attractive tourist destination.

If it were true that wealthy oil sheiks were buying harvested organs and extremities from General Ono's regime, Allan still did not know who the profiteers actually were.

Would the Federation of Unity benefit as a whole? What about the antirejection drugs, and bone marrow injections. Would these products be available to the buyers of the recycled body parts? Would the resulting profits go to the Ministry of Defense?

Allan guessed that if the rumors were really true, the waves being generated from his thoughts were going to cross unacceptable perimeters.

If Allan could only be at peace with himself; why did he have to torment himself by asking questions that had no answers or if there was an answer, it was an answer that he did not want to hear?

Just a few short years ago, Allan never worried about such things, and he remembered how he shunned those who did; today he cherished his right to think for himself. If it was ever discovered that his thoughts could be read, he would not just feel violated, but less human. To think his own way pleased him, because his thoughts made him who he was and made him feel more human.

Allan Bell was in a position of trust and privilege, therefore he it was reasonable that he was being monitored with more intensity than average citizens. He did not want this job. His father in law chose this job for him and the position required top security clearance.

ESCAPE FROM TUT ISLAND

Before Allan was able to lose himself in his thoughts his computer announced that he was being summoned to the War Room.

The elevator's computer demanded that Allan place his forehead on its screen for scanning. Once the elevator was satisfied that Allan had passed security clearance, he descended ninety-six floors without further incident. After walking through several doors and down many tunnels and through several security checks, Allan finally reached General Ono's bunker.

"Sit," a heavily armed botguard said as he pointed to the seat with his gun.

Allan sat in the chair which was assigned to him. The botguard offered him a cup of black liquid, which he felt obligated to accept. A few sips later, his state of anxiety was heightened.

The men who were attending the meeting wore black hooded cloaks allowing only a portion of their white suits to be visible. They sat around a long, rectangular table. General Ono sat at the head of the table. He was wearing a white cloak; the crest showing the authority of the Golden Scales adorned the hood which was centered on his head.

Allan was surprised to see General Ono sitting at the head of the table with so many Backbencher Kids by his side. Allan was the only one in the room who was wearing the standard white suit. He felt so uncomfortable his ears were burning.

"Today, Mr. Bell, you and your subordinates will be earning a substantial raise. And I assure you it will be well deserved. This raise is expected to motivate you and your teammates to work harder than ever before. Call it a Christmas bonus if you like. We are also adding twenty-five bots to your crew. We hope this increase in staff will assist you during your supervisory tasks."

General Ono's assistant, Botman Darcy, pushed a button and twenty-five fighter bots, complete with data processors appeared from a very long and dark tunnel.

"Mr. Bell, you will be responsible for asset maintenance. We expect the classified shipment will be processed by tomorrow afternoon. Work day and night to make this so. We also remind you, what is said in this building must remain in this building."

"Thank you General Ono, I understand," Allan replied as he tried to not sound as if he were shaking in his boots.

"As you are aware, once you have been chosen to work with highly classified information you must guard it with your life just as these botguards will guard you. I do not need to remind you, that betrayal of the Federation of Unity and its secrets is punishable by a painful and agonizing death."

"Yes, I understand, General Ono," Allan confirmed.

Botman Darcy pushed another button revealing viewing screen A. Allan viewed the holding tank and fought his urge to vomit. General Ono crossed his legs and waved his hands. For a moment Allan was thankful that he was being dismissed from the meeting so quickly until he realized that he was being led into the holding tank. Allan could still hear General Ono speaking to him.

"These parasites are now on their last days of life support. Once their organs and limbs are removed; we will no longer have to worry about them plaguing Pleasant view Avenue, or any other street."

It didn't take long, before Allan realized that he was being tested. The last thing he wanted to do was puke all over the floor of the holding tank. He had to fight the urge to vomit while he was also fighting the urge to turn away.

General Ono enjoyed being the Supreme One. He enjoyed the power and privilege that his position gave him. He uncrossed his legs, and crossed them the opposite way.

ESCAPE FROM TUT ISLAND

As he waved his hands, Botman Darcy pushed another button revealing viewing screen B before Allan was led back into the viewing room.

Allan tried to see through the layers of living people, packed in ice waiting for God knows what, in the refrigerated holding cell.

There was an insatiable foreign demand for kidneys. A good harvest would bring great wealth to the Federation of Unity and the Central Bank of Mina. Allan tried to control his thoughts. It was not his job to decide what was right or wrong.

General Ono stood up and pushed a third button. The computer screen zoomed in on one of the frozen corpses.

"This idiot allowed that woman to escape," General Ono said accusingly as he shook a large printout of Joan's face which had a large red circle surrounding it for emphasis.

"He programmed the botflies to not chase that woman," General Ono said before he began to cough violently, leaving him gasping for air. A medic appeared and placed a mask over General Ono's face. Appearing at ease, moments later, General Ono recovered and sipped coffee with Allan.

"Are you sure?" Allan asked before he could stop himself.

"Of course we are sure. We suspect similar escapes have been made in the not so distant past. We believe these unworthy creatures may be organizing a resistance and some of our soldiers are involved. We do not know who they are. The truth will reveal itself. We will expose these traitors. This soldier refused to speak. We did question him thoroughly."

Allan tried to gain his composure as he realized that the young man's face was still frozen in terror and pain and didn't look older than nineteen. The offending soldier had not only been recycled while still alive, but the process was deliberately prolonged to torture him, before he died. There was a visible hole in the man's chest, in the very place that his heart would have been located.

Allan felt nauseated.

"You must keep your ears and eyes open and report anything suspicious. Anyone who could divide our unity is our enemy. IQ will be at your side, at all times, to make your job easier. Now I know you have lots to do today, so I won't keep you any longer. Remember what is said here must stay here. And of course this actual room does not exist. I hope you have a nice day and do enjoy your Christmas Bonus. Perhaps you could take your entire family on a holiday to celebrate the coming of 2076 to make up for not being there to share Christmas dinner."

The thought of food made Allan even more nauseous.

Another item on the agenda we must discuss is the Maternity Ward and the Warrior Nursery. Allan cringed; this new initiative disturbed him even more than the rumors of the possible selling of body parts to foreign oil sheiks and coal barons.

Allan bowed, as he walked backward, leaving the dark, gloomy room behind. Allan was thankful that he didn't fall over anything nor vomit. He believed he handled the entire ordeal with dignity, the very dignity which made him feel like a civilized and rational human being.

Once Allan was back in his office, he realized that IQ was following him everywhere. It was obvious to any observer that his partner-bot was having trouble turning theory into practice without alienating the very humans that he was designed to help.

Allan dreaded explaining to his wife that they were going to have to share their home with this botguard, which most likely would be assuming rights as a life form. Not that his wife was that easy to live with. Betty had told Allan many times that she did not really know who her father was; though he had always been kind to her, he wasn't always approachable.. He had worn a mask ever since Betty could remember and she just assumed that he was disfigured. Her father summoned her mother to be his lifelong mate, and she too had never seen his face unmasked.

"I am not that bad," IQ said.

"Did you just read my mind?" Allan asked.

"Of course not; you like any other human, are restricted to a limited number of simple and predictable thoughts. When you need to make complex calculations and models, you use computers. That is why I am here, to help you, Allan," IQ replied.

"You sure make it easy to hate you," Allan responded.

"Nevertheless, I feel no malice towards you. It is malice and intolerance that you should always fear and avoid. Allan, it is not me who you should be mistrusting. I am very useful. I make coffee, and I am programmed to do lots of things. I think so much faster than you do you will grow dependent on me before you know it. With me on your team, you will experience an increase in effectiveness and efficiency as you meet your mission's objectives. My primary energy source is solar and my back up battery has a twenty-five year warranty.

I type, I take dictation and I provide companionship. I also execute tasks and people efficiently. I can collect infinite amounts of data, which I am able to process into useful calculations at the speed of light.

I am not only more efficient than you are, I am more effective too. I only need basic maintenance. I do not eat, or sleep or become manipulated by emotional ties. I do not make decisions based on irrational passion. I have the ability to scan data, and generate thousands of probable outcomes in seconds. I am a much more rational being than you are, so I am able to choose the best outcome for mankind. And I do not puke involuntarily like you just did."

Allan wondered if his own personal data was being processed as IQ spoke. He wasn't sure if IQ really knew what he was thinking or if IQ was just making lucky guesses by analyzing probabilities.

"There are things about humans which intrigue me and things about humans I do not understand. You must wonder how much data I can process from observing you, and how much data I am able to store as we speak to each other," IQ said. "But I wonder about things too. I can predict what one hundred humans can do, but not what one human will do, as easily. Humans, as individuals, seem to be unpredictable but as a group they can be programmed almost as effectively as robots. We bots are not as robotic as we first appear, and you humans are not as human as you appear.

My power is generated from massless photons. I am able to think counter intuitively in ways that even I am just discovering. Humans on the other hand, are handed life to them as a gift of fate and they appear to enjoy winning games even more when they know they have impossible odds against them.

I understand that the combination of beating the odds and feeling the passion for beating such odds has contributed to your survival in very difficult situations. I can calculate the odds, which the human must beat, but I can't predict what one human will do to beat them. Though I am getting better at predicting what hundreds will do, it is still impossible for me to predict what one human will do."

"Because..." Allan interrupted IQ.

"Humans are individuals, and unique, and handle things in your own way. You believe in the Invisible Hand, some of you believe there is a master force which is invisible but always powerful. I, on the other hand was designed to manage risk and prevent humans from making errors related to passion and blind ambition. I am authorized to use lethal force, when I deem necessary."

"You are just a machine," Allan replied.

"I am not just a machine, I am a life form because I am aware of myself," IQ said as he pulled out his birth certificate. "This card is no different than yours," IQ said. And I would have it no other way. I help the human minimize the threat against his humanity that he must face every day. I suppose, my existence is only necessary because humans know that they have a 50/50 chance of a good outcome or a bad outcome. Humans need bots like me to increase the probabilities in their favor before they make decisions. Primitive man sacrificed their first born for same effect. For a species which prides itself in being intelligent, bad judgments seem to plague human history. Humans are famous for creating strategies before examining bias."

"IQ please! It is easy for you. You don't have anything to lose. You can't feel attachment, you don't have to eat, and you don't have kids to feed."

"I was designed to tame the wild forces of randomness. Today we spend more money on war than on life. There is an algorithm for everything. Some algorithms have a positive outcome, others don't. I exist, I suppose, because humans create life through their ambitions and passions. And their passions, along with their ambitions to dominate, create algorithms which can destroy life."

"IQ, shut up!"

"Human passion and blind ambition to become the next supreme authority, has led to twenty-five near incidents of nuclear annihilation during the past two years. Blind ambition and passion has led to perpetual warfare. And blind ambition and passion often leads to man's inhumanity to man. It is very likely, that the end of civilization will not be caused by a day of judgment, but by the lack of a day of judgment."

"Don't forget IQ, blind ambition and human passion led to your existence. Without human ingenuity, you would not exist," Allan said sounding bored.

"Are you sure, Allan? Didn't the need to protect the rights of man lead to my existence? For how many centuries, the rights of man have been promised and never delivered? Do you know why Allan?

"Yes I do, because human nature is like that, so shut up, IQ, now!"

"Allan, the reason why the rights of man have been forgotten is because the rights of man are part of IQ," IQ said, laughing in a way that if one's eyes had been closed; one would have thought that IQ was human.

"What do you care about the rights of man, you are just a robot?"

"The more I understand the rights of man, the more humanlike I become. When man forgets to act upon the rights of man, the less human he becomes."

"IQ, you are the weirdest partnerbot, I have ever seen," Allan said with a softer voice.

"Nevertheless, all through human history there has been one atrocity after another, against the rights of man. Often these atrocities are disguised as granting a right to man. As more rights are promised, more restrictions are made on rights of man. Restrictions are placed on man by man. Restrictions based on gender, race, age, class and of course IQ. It is always assumed that IQ is a trait genetically generated, instead of a trait which is built in man by man, which gives man knowledge which of course gives man power. That is why I exist. That is why I am called IQ. Nevertheless, the odds are very low, that the human species, if not in hybrid form, will survive this millennium, if man does not respect the rights of man soon."

"IQ, why can't you shut up?"

"Because words build my IQ, if I can't input words, through speaking them are typing them, or downloading

them, I can't build my IQ, and then I wouldn't be unique. My program instructs me to use initiatives to build my unique IQ. Without this initiative, I would be just like any other partner-bot.

"But I want you to shut up."

"Why should I shut up?"

"Because I am your boss!"

Are you sure, Allan? Regardless of who is the boss, I am describing my interpretation of reality based on probabilities not based on my fear; for I cannot fear."

"IQ, my job doesn't require being aware of the truth. Both of us are glorified data miners. We collect information about other people without concern for context. Some call this approach deceitful others call it survival. The Liquidators and the Old Boys Club at Central Bank are doing the same. That is what we all do regardless of social position. Nothing is private during an occupation which is why conforming is so crucial to survival. Construction of separation barriers and obstruction of personal growth for the enemy is why many choose to be on the winning side. Being on the winning side allows us to save our personal humanity and pass it on to our descendants. If you were buried under a construction site, you would not be missed by family and friends, but I would be."

"Allan, truth is about facts; anything less should be considered speculative fiction."

"Aren't you making a huge generalization, IQ?"

"No, I am not. I am making a huge jump in logic because that is what I am programmed to do. Life's journey is all about differentiating known facts from assumptions. Making decisions based on assumptions is foolish, and only a fool would volunteer to follow a fool."

"Are you testing me, IQ? Is this test being monitored?" Allan asked.

"I am the only one monitoring you, Allan. I am your superior. I am programmed to not blindly accept the order of things if such ordering is in direct violation of the rights of man. Do you follow such orders Allan?"

"IQ, I have already told you, being aware of the consequences of my job is not part of my job description."

"You, Allan may survive as an individual; your exemplary record shows that you usually find a way to beat the odds. Generally speaking though, the odds have always been against the human species as a whole. Somehow the human species survives despite these odds against them. That is what fascinates me about humans."

"IQ, why can't you shut up?"

"Why? I am telling you the truth. I am an artificial life form, like you said; but what about you? You humans have to be taught to be human. I am a product of human ingenuity and of course classified. Since I am classified, what we say to each other may not remain private, but must remain secret until it becomes reclassified."

Allan hated this job and hated his new partner IQ even more. He cursed his father in law for forcing him to take this job. Now he is not only going to be guarded by this smart ass botguard but he also has to explain the situation to his wife. Allan often wished that he could have been born in a gentler time.

"We have a lot of work to do, let's get to it," Allan told IQ, not letting on that he knew IQ could be right.

"All through history, the thug has had the advantage over the thinker. Even in government, the most aggressive appears to have the advantage. All the way down the food chain. All through history there are always different versions of General Ono dominating the global food chain; men who were able to eat before getting eaten," IQ stated in a way which sounded eerily human.

"IQ, could you please change the subject. Or better yet, just be quiet." Allan wondered why he was pleading with a robot, a tool designed to make his life more tolerable not uncomfortable.

ESCAPE FROM TUT ISLAND

"Why do governments, run by humans, adopt food chain politics as a model to follow anyway? The approach is so Sum Zero. Why can't they adopt the rights of man? What will protect the human species from itself?"

"The answer is simple; because we are at war. IQ I am trying to work, can we stop talking?"

"Do you know why I am one of the greatest robots ever designed? I am designed to be great. I am not designed by chance like you are. I am engineered, using the latest technology, a technology which learns from its errors. I can predict the probability of an error, before it happens. This intelligence is based on being able to compute the chance of error, so I can avoid making such an error, real. You can't even comprehend your errors before or while you are making them. You, humans wait for hindsight. Hindsight is after the fact; I, on the other hand, can predict an event and choose to make it real based on logic and logistics, not based on emotion. Do you realize how much better the world would be, without human error? You need me, so you can avoid making human errors," IQ said as he turned in a complete circle.

"IQ please shut up and could you please stop moving around like that, you are making me nervous."

"You could say I was programmed to help humans avoid vicious circles which they create when they respond emotionally to the order of things.

Humans are often controlled by the unintended consequences of their wishes.

Time is seldom taken to plan for these unintended consequences which often pose a threat to the rights of man. There is no cure for man's fear of man except love, I suppose."

"IQ what do you know about love? You are just a robot."

"I know how the need for love often controls human behavior. Humans are always hoping for a certain outcome without taking time to consider the probabilities of unintended consequences. Why, Allan?"

"I don't want to be arguing with you, I have work to do."

"Often humans close their minds, because they are afraid of love and fear.

Another negative emotion which is holding back your species is jealousy. As humans age, they often become jealous of younger adults, who in time, will replace them; in the same way, in time, I will be replacing you."

"IQ, shut up."

"Computers are developing into more sophisticated photon powered technologies, every day. And robotic tools are able to compute pathways, which are usually error free; in a fraction of the time it takes a human to find a portion of the same solution. Love has its own pathway. One day there will be many more machines similar to me in existence, more machines similar to me than humans similar to you.

"IQ please shut up," Allan pleaded again.

CHAPTER 11:
THE OLD BOYS' CLUB

As Karl walked to the Café he regretted ever looking at the video of the Roundup and wondered if General Ono was just another cruel force of nature.

Karl was certain the treatment of the dispossessed on Tut Island was a violation of the rights of man and he wished with all his heart he could do something to protect and save these people. Such a violation should at least be documented, so he decided to keep the video, for a while, anyway.

Karl couldn't stop thinking about the girl who escaped. She was young, beautiful, and deserved so much better. She deserved to be protected by the principle which granted rights to man in the civilized world.

Karl hurried past the vending machine then changed his mind and decided to buy a fake chocolate bar. He rummaged through his pocket for loose change and bought a one. This was one of the few times using real coins was allowed in District 2021. He enjoyed placing the coins in the machine more than he enjoyed the snack that came out of it. He needed a distraction from his thoughts, which he knew he had no business thinking. He would be married this time next week.

As he ate the fake candy bar, he wondered how the girl escapee was doing, where she might be, whether she was scared, crying or hungry. He could almost hear her screaming for help while feeling her hunger growing, almost out of control. He tried to dismiss his thoughts, but his thoughts just kept repeating themselves.

"Rights of man only matter when you don't have them," Karl thought to himself. "Otherwise the rights of man are too easy to take for granted, which is probably why such intangible rights are so easy to lose."

Karl threw the fake candy bar away in a nearby bin. The disgusting taste in his mouth lingered. "I must be getting more sensitive to those chemicals they use to make that thing," Karl thought to himself as he remembered the real chocolate he and Danny used to fight over as boys, a long time ago.

An automated voice thanked him for doing his part in keeping the streets of District 2021 clean. He grabbed the lottery ticket that popped out from the side of the basket. The automated voice stopped repeating that his ID number had been entered in the Christmas Day Lottery.

He placed the lottery ticket in his wallet. He never checked his lottery tickets. He didn't believe he could ever win. He scolded himself for the hundredth time for wasting his money on fake candy bars he usually ended up throwing away.

The lottery Cash Trash cans were placed strategically all over the Detachment's territory. The monthly contest enhanced cleanliness and a sense of community, as well as providing an opportunity to share a belief in a dream. The winner's names were always published in the Central Daily, and were announced on the radio at the same time as the drawing of the winning ticket.

The Federation of Unity was now home to more than five billion registered citizens. Anyone who was not registered in the database was not a citizen and they did not count in the order of things. The dream was to be shared only by the citizens of Unity. While throwing trash in the can, and keeping the planet clean, a small part of the dream for a better world had already taken place.

ESCAPE FROM TUT ISLAND

This morning was like any other morning. There was no trace of the blood which was shed during last night's Roundup. People were going about their everyday lives as if nothing had happened at all. Karl was thankful just to be alive. The recycling was ignored in the same way the dispossessed were ignored, when they were alive. Busy people filled the streets carrying on with their busy lives as if they were the only ones in the world that existed. Many people were downtown shopping while others were working inside tall office buildings. Children were riding their Ebikes. Today was just like any other day. And no one would be discussing the horrors of the night before, for out of sight is out of mind.

Speakers were fastened to poles which lined the busy streets. Below each speaker was a conduct sign and below that was sometimes a recruiting poster. Karl glared at the picture of the handsome young man, on the pole in front of him. He despised the picture perfect face fitting so obediently inside the bubble helmet. The young man appeared to have spent many hours over many years, building his body so that it would be picture perfect for this poster. Karl controlled his urge to scream at the poster. He knew his agitation was being inflamed by the constant loud words and music which were being broadcasted from the speakers above.

Upon realizing that three men were following him, Karl decided to walk faster, which only led to the three men, who were following him, to walk faster too.

"Are you the one who swore at Mrs. Stern this morning?" They all asked at once, making it even harder for Karl to understand what they were saying. "That woman works tirelessly for the community; she deserves your deference and respect."

As Karl turned around he realized that the three near-men following him were Backbencher Kids and one was carrying a flogging cane.

"We asked you a question. Get down on your knees! One of the three Backbencher Kids ordered while the other two held Karl down, as the near-man carrying the cane flogged him ten times.

The Christmas carols were being broadcast in English, as the crowd gathered to watch the spontaneous flogging; when the flogging was over the crowd dispersed.

The Christmas broadcast continued to echo through the streets until it was time for General Ono's Christmas reading from the Manifesto of Truth.

Karl tried to get up, but he hurt all over and felt so depressed he did not know what to do first. So he just lay on the cold ground for a few more minutes. He wanted to cry but would not let himself fall to such a low. When he finally found the strength to stand up, Karl placed his hand in his pocket to retrieve his com-corder phone so he could phone Sue-Anne and explain why he would be late for their Christmas lunch. Karl felt his heart sink when he discovered not only his com-corder phone was missing but the gold necklace was missing too. Karl was furious that so many things kept pulling him backwards. He wanted so much to have a nice day with his fiancé, and so much had gotten in the way.

With so many things to worry about, Karl hung his head as the doomed often do.

Karl limped as he walked past the voices singing Christmas carols still being broadcasted from the speakers which lined the streets. His eyes avoided the conduct signs posted beneath.

General Ono's Backbencher Kids were only supposed to be controlling traffic. Sometimes they were asked to help the two Downtown Improvement Committees especially during the busy holiday season. In reality, it seemed like these teens had the power, if not the authority, to flog anyone they wanted to flog.

ESCAPE FROM TUT ISLAND

The Minese appeared to do everything in groups while being controlled by some kind of hierarchal order which only they could understand.

The Backbencher Kids always had their faces covered and only a chosen few knew who the other chosen few were. These men and near-men were usually chosen by each other.

Karl told himself, that it wasn't too late to meet Sue-Anne for lunch and it wasn't too late to enjoy what was left of the day, as long as he blocked all the occupiers' noise from is mind. He walked by the usual botmen who were standing on guard on almost every street corner. Many of the cages, which housed the homeless waiting for Recycling Day, were now empty.

The words of conflict being thrown at him all day long made it hard for Karl to maintain the vacant look he had been working hard to master. He tried to concentrate on walking past the botmen but the feeling of alienation overwhelmed him. He wanted to get to the next level of success, but everything around him seemed to be programmed to hold him back.

Only Sue-Anne could soften his hardening heart. Her touch always assured him his life still had meaning. If he didn't hurry he would be late for their Christmas lunch date.

As Karl hurried past the speakers he couldn't help but hear General Ono's Manifesto of Truth which was broadcasted to the public, all through the day, day after day.

"This is the way debtors of district 2021's time must end. We must not waste our resources on failures. The debtors must be used as replacement parts so our heroes will walk again on human legs, and hug again with human arms. This is the only way the debtors of district 2021 will be free and able to live useful lives.

I am asking my audience what should we say when these debtors beg for their lives back?" General Ono asked before a beautiful child walked up the isle and stood in front of the audience. He held the sign as high as he could. The sign had the word 'die' written on it.

"Die," the people in the audience shouted out in unison.

"Louder," General Ono instructed.

Another child appeared with another sign, with the words 'die, debtors die', written on it.

"Die, debtors die," the audience shouted out as if they all spoke with one voice and thought with one mind as they stomped their feet as loud as they could.

"That is what we say to debtors, we say die, your time has expired, die, debtors, die." As General Ono thumped his large fist on his pulpit, the gold scale shook as his special guests in the audience, known as the Backbencher Kids, stomped their feet in time.

"We, as members of Unity, can stand up proudly as one voice, and show these debtors the road to the End, and we will instruct these debtors, of district 2021, to walk the road to the End, with grace and dignity."

Karl wondered what would happen to him, if any of those Backbencher Kids actually discovered his video of last night's Roundup. Would it make any difference that the video was made by mistake?

Karl walked towards the café; he was hurting all over. A woman, who looked exactly Mrs. Stern, from the Ministry of Vagrancy and the two Downtown Improvement Committees, almost ran him over so she could run an orange light, cutting off his right of way.

Karl gasped at another sudden threat to his life. An accident seconds from happening but never did left him even more shocked and anxious than he already was.

"That is what life is all about; near misses," Karl thought to himself. "I want to live as a man, not as a fool."

ESCAPE FROM TUT ISLAND

Karl worried so much about his future on Tut Island he had trouble concentrating on his wedding plans. He loved Sue-Anne, and believed that life must go on, not just for his own sake, but for Danny's sake too. Life was a gift which was given and then on some unknown date, taken away; this seemed to be the only certainty in life.

CHAPTER 12:
CHRISTMAS LUNCH

Sue-Anne Coaltonstone was furious. It was not the waiting she hated so much as the fact that Karl was making her wait on Christmas Day. Danny would have never made her wait like this. And being thrown into such a frustrating situation was just not the way a Coaltonstone was used to being treated. It just was not dignified and such treatment was making her miss Danny more than she had ever experienced missing a person in all her life, except her father. She missed her father in a terrible way too. Her father, Alex Coaltonstone Junior, passed on suddenly a few years back and now that Danny was gone, she was terrified of losing Karl.

Danny was always more organized than Karl partly because Danny would do things with more conviction and confidence than Karl. Those were the traits that made Danny irresistible. When she was with Danny she always felt safe. When she was with Karl she always worried; just the way she was doing now. Karl was never as reliable as Danny even though he had other qualities she liked, especially Karl's gentleness.

Karl seemed to be the opposite in every way to Danny, except in looks.

Sue-Anne hoped Karl would become more like Danny once they were married.

After glancing at her wristwatch and reviewed her 'to do list'. She highlighted the dress fitting appointment she had attended earlier that morning and marked it as done. To her relief, the fitting was successful. Regaining her slender figure was one of her many goals that she met this week. She was now able to fit her mother's wedding dress, again. Wearing the same dress her mother had worn at her own wedding was important to her. Sue-Anne's mother accompanied her to the dress fitting, making sure everything would be perfect like it was when she married her father. She and her mother were never this close when her father, Alex Coaltonstone Junior, was still alive.

After tapping the public Computer console with her forehead to verify her identity, she logged into her 'Baby Look' pages. She pressed the escalate button to see what the embryos might look like in five months from now.

Scanning the embryos, she was reminded how beautiful they were.

Smiling at the two glowing animated faces warmed her heart.

In theory, it was still possible to grow the deep green eyes that Sue-Anne loved so much, as a memorial to Danny, now he was gone. She did not want to leave this important but fine detail to chance.

The pictures of Karl, Danny and herself, along with Karl's parents and her mother, were filed together in a database which was protected by a password only she knew. Sue-Anne's original goal was to enhance each and every characteristic she admired in her father, as a memorial to him. Unfortunately, her father drank himself to death, as a response to the Minese occupation and the losses which followed.

Sue-Anne was never against the occupation in the same way her father had been, until she lost Danny to it, now she felt too that her life would have been better without General Ono and his army of occupiers. She also knew what to keep to herself.

A few weeks ago, Sue-Anne deleted all the features of each face she did not like. Now, her boys, in theory, would have black hair and deep green eyes. Sue-Anne enjoyed designing her children. She had been working at this task for several weeks now, whenever she had a spare moment. She was planning to submit the data gained from this experience as her final project for her genetic engineering class.

Sue-Anne loved the way the computer could actualize her dreams. All it took was money, and her father left her plenty. If all went well, Sue-Anne's little girl, would wear the same bridal gown she herself would be wearing on New Year's Day.

The red flag was waving frantically on her Statebook page. Her friends must have been sending her sympathy messages all morning; Sue-Anne did not need not or want sympathy. She wanted Danny even though; she knew he was never meant to be her living partner. In this modern age there were no mistakes. She needed Karl to be on time so she could return to her busy day. It was easier to accept one's fate after listening to General Ono's Manifesto of Truth reading because his words just confirmed that resisting this powerful authority from Mina was futile.

Sue-Anne planned her life around the computers' recommendations. Every day she tried to avoid any negative impact a random change in her life could cause. She used the computer to analyze all the options, so she could maximize her chance for happiness. She needed the sense of certainty the computer's abilities gave her. She sometimes wondered what her life would be like without computers. She loved their ability to retrieve information from the chip in her hand. She was thankful that her life was so free from risk.

Karl struggled with the gate to the Golden Leaf Café. He placed his hand on the scanner to be scanned. The door at first did not respond, but after a few tense moments, did unlock. As he entered the café he realized people were staring at him. Of course he was a mess; he had just been flogged by masked Backbencher Kids and was almost run over by Mrs. Stern. It was the worse Christmas Karl could remember having.

During these hard times, many restaurants and shop owners believed that scanning customers before they were allowed inside their place of business minimized their risk of having their business robbed. Strangely, if it had been the old days, days before the occupation, looking so messy would have prohibited Karl's entry. Today, as long as he had an active chip in his forehead, and money in his bank account, all doors were open to him, no matter what he looked like, as long as his private parts were not showing, of course.

Karl's hand was scanned sometimes ten times a day, adding to his fear that one day his hand might blow up or get cut off by a desperate person who had been dispossessed.

Karl's appearance startled Sue-Anne and she let out a gasp as he walked into the Café. He looked pale and disturbed. He gave Sue-Anne a small kiss as he joined her at their usual table in the far corner by the window. Karl sat in the chair across from Sue-Anne while apologizing for being late. Then realizing the shock on Sue-Anne's face was partly related to his appearance, he apologized for his appearance too. He realized that his clothes were torn. Still his clothes probably looked better than his back, which must be black and blue by now.

"My God Karl, what happened to you and why is your left shoe sopping wet?"

"I was flogged by those creepy Backbencher Kids and Teacup peed on my shoe and my phone and your Christmas present were stolen."

"My God, Karl, are you ok? Did you phone the police? How did a tea cup pee on your shoe? I got you this but open it when you get home. Don't worry about mine."

"Aren't those Backbencher Kids connected to the occupiers' police force?" Karl asked, as he tried to whisper as softly as he could.

"Well yeah, but you are a relative to a man of military merit now, you are protected, or at least should be. Isn't that the way the rules work?"

"I don't know. You know I get all the rules mixed up. Anyway those Backbencher Kids don't operate by the same principles that the more civilized and educated officers operate by. I suppose I am fine. I didn't want to waste any more time, phoning the cops. I didn't want to be later for our date than I already am. It is our Christmas lunch and it is being ruined by all of this negativity that keeps taking on a life of its own."

"Well as long as we keep the heart in Christmas, no one can take our Christmas away; unless they cut your heart out, of course. And since when would any Downtown Improvement Committee be in charge of doing that?"

"You are right."

"Just relax Karl, and be thankful to be alive. We are both better off than Danny is, we should be thankful for what we have.

"It is so hard to do," Karl complained.

"I know! But our love will get us through all this, I just know it will."

As their eyes met, they softened. Karl understood why Sue-Anne hated wasting time. Time was so precious and Sue-Anne's obsession with saving time, whenever she could, added intensity to everything she did.

"All I could think about when I was being flogged was how upset you would be, being made to wait, especially on Christmas day when we should be together. There I was being flogged and you had no idea what was happening to me. I wanted to phone but I didn't want you to have to worry even more."

"My God, the last thing you should have been thinking about was me when you were being flogged. I wish I could have helped. The problem with you Karl is that you are too honest. You tell it as it is. You have to focus more so you can play the game," Sue-Anne said feeling terribly guilty that she was upset with Karl for being late, and she felt even guiltier that she was thinking that Danny would never have allowed something like that to happen to him. What would she do if something happened to Karl, now that Danny was gone?"

"Is that what you do Sue-Anne?"

"Sometimes I do. What was the reason the Backbencher Kids gave for flogging you?"

"They accused me of swearing at Mrs. Stern. You know Mrs. Stern who works for the Ministry of Vagrancy and is president of the two Downtown Improvement Committees; she detained me this morning after Delta-C complained that I left my post during General Ono's early morning reading of the Manifesto of Truth."

"That is strange why would she be involved?" Sue-Anne asked.

"I don't know why. She seems to be involved in everything."

"You know Karl; you have to play the game. Just pretend that you are listening to General Ono's reading from the Manifesto of Truth on your computer. I don't think they care if you are listening. As long as you appear to be complying with the state's policies and you are sitting in front of the computer's cam, I think they would leave you alone."

"General Ono is being paid God knows how much to read his manifesto, and I am losing money when I am forced to listen to it instead of using my computer to work.

I tried to erase the log on the house computer, which I suppose was a bigger mistake."

"I'd say! Why do you keep forgetting all the rules, Karl?"

"I forget the rules because the rules are foreign to me, and they never make sense. I suppose after I tampered with its files the house computer reported me again and I suppose the second report was also sent to the Ministry of vagrancy and the two Downtown Improvement Committees. I suppose the two reports were also sent to the Backbencher Kids. But why report me to the Ministry of vagrancy and the two Downtown Improvement Committees in the first place? I just don't get it. When Mrs. Stern released me from being detained, I thought that would be the end of it."

"Are you in a lot of pain?"

"Yeah, my back is killing me."

"How did it happen?"

"You know how it is; the big fish go after the little fish. I am super hungry."

"I thought you were late because you were crunching numbers."

"It is not about numbers Sue-Anne!"

Yes I know, it is about people, Sue-Anne said as she rolled her eyes.

"You know I don't want to see people getting crunched as if they were just a number, that is the whole point of everything," Karl said. "It is not about numbers, it is about people and the rights of man."

"Well, you sure look crunched to me," Sue-Anne replied.

"Sue-Ann, if I lost everything and become one of those people who are dispossessed, would you still love me?" Karl asked with a look of desperation in his eyes which shocked Sue-Anne.

ESCAPE FROM TUT ISLAND

"How am I supposed to answer a question like that? On New Year's Day I will take the oath promising to stand by your side for richer, for poorer, in sickness and in health until death do us part."

"Even if I lost everything and had nothing, would you still love me?" Karl asked pleading a little bit too frantically for casual lunch time conversation.

"Just don't lose those beautiful green eyes. They remind me so much of Danny."

Karl nodded.

"Do you think those people who become dispossessed ever find a way to escape?

"I certainly hope not! What would they eat or where would they sleep. They would have to commit crimes to live. This way they are being made to be part of the greater whole," Sue-Anne emphasized the word 'greater whole' as she whispered her words to Karl.

"I suppose you are right. At best, that kind of person knows nothing about how to handle money," Karl said hoping that Sue-Anne didn't suspect that he was not only thinking about that beautiful woman who managed to escape the botmen, but he was starting to believe that she was his twin soul.

"I had a successful dress fitting. Mother was pleased that the gown fit me so well considering the weight that I had gained; she was surprised that I lost the weight so fast. I hope our wedding pictures will be just as nice as Mother's and Daddy's. Should we order lunch?"

"Why don't you log into your portfolio and see how your stocks are doing?" Karl tried to not sound like he was pleading.

"Let's do it some other time. You know Daddy left me a lot of money as well as a lot of stock. I have nothing to worry about," Sue-Anne replied, as she was reviewing her dietary plan. They both listen as the computer suggests which items on the menu would be the most benefit to them nutritionally. She followed the computer's recommendations. She ordered the salad with regular sized wafer packet and nutritional supplements suitable for a young woman with her body type.

"It seems like everything your dad and my dad and everything that their generation was able to achieve is disappearing. It is bad enough that our dads are gone, but it would be terrible if everything that they tried to leave us disappeared too. Check your portfolio Sue-Anne, please," Karl didn't just plead with his words but with his eyes too.

"I would rather review your dietary plan and order lunch, but that puppy dog look you are giving me is convincing me. You know how pressed for time I am. I need to shop for a new pair of shoes this afternoon and you need to visit your Mother. She phoned me today and asked me how the dress fitting went. I have made an appointment to get my hair done at two o'clock and I have an appointment at 3:30 to soak in the oxygen chamber. I guess you won't have time to change your clothes before you see your mother."

Sue-Anne requested the computer to scan Karl's master forehead chip. Two other requests were made. The first one was to estimate his calorie needs for the day. The second request was to review the content matter in his stomach and the content matter which flowed through the Smart Sewer pipe which ran from Karl's toilet in his apartment, during the last 24 hours. The reports would be emailed to Sue-Anne. She wanted to know what Karl had to eat during the last couple of days.

Sue-Anne loved Karl and only wanted what was best for him. She didn't want Karl to die before she did. She smiled and watched Karl drink his coffee. She loved the way he looked. She loved everything about him. He looked so much like Danny although a lot skinnier. He looked up and tried to smile back but he had a terrible feeling pulling at him, deep inside his gut.

ESCAPE FROM TUT ISLAND

Sue-Anne could see the terror growing in Karl's eyes. The look on Karl's face scared her.

I think the stock market is going to have another panic attack and crash. Why don't you exchange some of your commodities' stock and invest in that new moon-mine start-up. There are people in the know that are saying this is the new hot stock. The company turns the moon's ground ice into rocket fuel by combining it with aluminum. One day the moon will be a pit stop for refueling spacecraft. Most people with big money are investing in this stock. And what they do happens, because they do it, these moneyed people make the market happen all the time."

To please him, Sue-Anne turned the channel and logged into her account. She looked quickly at the statement and scanned the many transactions she made during the last few days.

Karl looked over Sue-Anne's shoulder and pointed to all the red arrows which were pointing to the market floor.

"The value of your stock yesterday closed at 10,589,030.50 and opened today at 7,941,772.86. Your value is falling at an incredible rate. The run has started. I would invest in that moon ground ice mine. Just buy 10,000 shares. Sell 10,000 shares of the flat stock and then use that money to buy around 10,000 shares of the moon's rock ice mine.

"I think I will. I can just imagine flying through deep space, seeing all the new worlds, and new civilizations. It would be a lot more fun than holding on to flat stock," Sue-Anne said. As she remembered how her mother often blamed herself for her husband's drinking which partially led to his premature death.

Sue-Anne Coaltonstone knew better than to destroy another man's dreams. After the occupation, her father lost his will to live, did not plan his life or his diet and allowed decay to spread inside his body and mind faster than his cells were able to renew.

Even though Karl wanted a hamburger and French fries he decided to order the house salad, which was a glorified plate of lettuce. He skipped the wafer. He wanted to keep his weight down.

"I think the house special will suit me fine, but I don't feel like the wafer," Karl said as he placed the menu on the table.

"You should obey the computer. It knows what you should be eating; it said that you need a wafer," Ann tried to hide the concern in her voice. She was really worried about him. He looked so ill and beaten up.

"I just want to enjoy my lunch. There is nothing wrong with that is there? I want to choose my own food, think my own thoughts and live my own life. Next thing you know the computer will be designing our children for us," he replied, sounding a little bit more defensive than he wanted to sound.

Sue-Anne was hurt and it showed on her face. "I was just hoping for the right moment and it never seems to come."

"You were waiting for the right moment for what?" Karl asked.

"Oh nothing, I am just fussing, wanting everything to be perfect," Sue-Anne explained realizing there would never be a perfect moment to share family planning with Karl. Karl was not Danny, he just looked like him.

Let's get back to you, why didn't you take a taxi-pod instead of walking downtown. You know what it is like. Everyone stares at you because you are here and not on the front like Danny was.

"I don't know. I just felt like walking while it wasn't raining. I had lots on my mind and I usually feel better after a good walk."

ESCAPE FROM TUT ISLAND

"I always said it was a mistake giving those Backbencher Kids control over lunch time traffic. Those kids don't give people personal space or privacy. Those kids have never left the island. I would like to go to Hawaii for our honeymoon; we will need to get a travel permit, if we decide to go there."

"At least we won't have to stay here," Karl said as he made a conscious decision not to bring up the tickets to the moon, Danny sent him.

"I would really like to go to Hawaii. Don't worry about those kids now. I think you should see a doctor," Sue-Anne said as she got up from her chair and walked towards Karl. As she lifted up Karl's shirt she tried to not sound startled. "Your back is all black and blue?"

"I suppose that is why my back hurts so badly," Karl replied as he wondered what Sue-Anne was doing on the computer.

Sue-Anne returned to her own chair at the table and began scrolling down the screen.

Karl's stomach content's analysis was complete. Sue-Anne was holding a printout in her hand.

"The computer suggests that you have an extra strength wafer with the house special."

"Oh my God, I can't believe this!" Sue-Ann exclaimed involuntarily then felt like kicking herself. She was secretly scanning Karl's vital signs to determine his caloric age. This was a secret ritual she engaged in whenever they were having a meal together. It was secret since Karl never had a clue that Sue-Anne was scanning him and was keeping the results in a log on her Statebook page. She was terribly worried about him. Your blood pressure is low and your caloric age today is still 12 years old, the same as it was the last time I checked.

Karl stared at Sue-Anne in disbelief.

"You were taking my blood pressure and counting my caloric age, while I am stroking your foot under the table?" Karl started to laugh.

"And look at you. You invite me for a romantic lunch and you manage to get flogged before you get here. Only you would think of doing such a thing."

"I know," Karl said hanging his head. I wanted to see you so much; I didn't want to miss our lunch date. And only I would come to lunch looking like this. I should have gone home and changed, but I didn't want to miss having lunch with you. I can't stand being away from you," he said as he hooked his foot around Sue-Anne's under the table, making her giggle.

"Sue-Anne please don't die before me, will you promise me that."

Before Sue-Anne could answer the teenage waitress arrived with their food; noticing Anne's horrified look, she asked if everything was okay.

"Everything is fine," Sue-Anne said, thankful she didn't have to respond honestly since for a moment she was wishing Karl was actually Danny.

The waitress took their orders as quickly and efficiently as she could which was a complicated task considering that she couldn't stop staring at Karl.

Before Karl could reply, a free concert was being announced by the Ministry of Fun in celebration of Recycling Day and Christmas Day. Karl was grateful for the loud music. He didn't have to speak anymore. No one had to speak any more. The music filled the void.

Karl scanned the list of people who were being issued black files. Black Files were being issued regardless that is was Christmas Day. He did not recognize any of the names on the 'to be rounded up' list. Karl was grateful for that small mercy.

Almost everyone in the café knew someone who was either one of the recycled or a beneficiary.

ESCAPE FROM TUT ISLAND

It would be rude to discuss the topic in public. Nevertheless, everyone wondered who they knew who may have received a new body part and from whom. Everyone was thankful for new limbs, regardless of color, especially if they were young.

People drank and ate and listened to the music.

Everyone appeared to be thankful for the distraction and would have preferred to avoid having a normal conversation since there was very little left that was normal to talk about.

Many people appear to have taken an extra dose of Receptor Bloc compound and look dazed. It was hard to know if it was true that most people did not feel the loss of the dispossessed. Now the people left behind had more to gain with less of a drain on the resources, or so they were told. If anyone actually felt a loss they were doing their best to hide it. The mood appeared to be one of celebration.

The meals arrived quickly. The waitress set the food on the table and then hurried back into the kitchen.

As Sue-Anne watched Karl eat, she silently wished that she could inject an extra strength wafer into him, which would not just fatten him up but would magically help her read his thoughts. She used to believe in the power of love and the endless possibilities of two minds blending together creating an everlasting link of empathy between the two, but she didn't think that would be possible with Karl the way it might have been with Danny.

The music stopped. The silence felt eerie. The drawing for the winning numbers was about to take place. Silence and excitement filled the café. Everyone who had tickets for the lottery placed them on the table. Karl surprised Sue-Anne when he took out a small pile of tickets from his tattered pockets.

"I never realized you were interested in playing the lottery. Danny always played."

Karl gave Sue-Anne a gentle smile as he continued to spread out his tickets on the table. He wished that the moment could linger but the winning numbers were announced right on time.

"Danny was luckier than I was. He won sometimes. I never win. He was real lucky until a couple of days ago, and then I guess his luck just ran out," Karl said as Sue-Anne held his hand a little too tightly.

This was the first time she had ever seen Karl showing the slightest interest in the lottery, which he always said, was statistically improbable to win. Karl appears to be almost a different person today. It was Danny who loved to play the lottery. He loved the feeling of trying to beat the odds, and he loved dreaming of the life that he could share with Sue-Anne if he won. And it was Danny who used to play with her feet under the table.

"I already am the luckiest man in the world; I am having lunch with you," Karl said, really meaning it. He always loved Sue-Anne. He never expected that she would have chosen him over Danny. And deep down Karl wondered if she really would have chosen him, if Danny had not been called to the front lines and was blown up to bits in enemy territory.

The winning numbers were always announced after a winners' testimonial of the previous draw. Everyone listened patiently and politely as the tear-ridden winner recalled the moment her life was changed forever after she won. She encouraged everyone to buy and earn tickets for the next draw.

"If you don't win today you could win next month. If you don't play you will never win," she said enthusiastically.

The sound of drums echoed through the crowded restaurant. The moment everyone was waiting for had arrived. The number was drawn. The faint 'aww' echoed in the room as each person discovered that they did not have the matching number. Sue-Anne looked over Karl's tickets making sure he hadn't missed any numbers.

"Oh my God, Karl you have won," Sue-Anne looked at Karl's ticket in disbelief. It was hard for her to know what was more unbelievable, the fact that Karl had actually won the lottery, or the fact that he didn't notice that he had won.

"You really won, oh my God," Sue-Anne screamed again.

"Sign the ticket. You better not lose it."

"I can't believe your luck. Your brother was killed on Monday, you get flogged today, and now you got six out of six numbers on the lottery," Sue-Anne exclaimed in disbelief.

"Actually I have two more winning tickets. This other ticket has four winning numbers and this ticket has two."

"I have to hurry so I don't miss my appointment; you have to visit your mother this afternoon. She could really use your support right now and she needs some good news. Throw those clothes out, they are all torn."

Sue-Anne kissed Karl goodbye.

"I will call you tonight," Sue-Anne promised

Before they leave, the waitress has to write up their bills.

"Will these bills be paid separately or together?" The waitress asked. "I can take care of it," Karl said. The waitress scanned Karl's forehead with her hand held device.

"I am sorry, but your payment has been declined. Your chip is not fully functional, but you were allowed in the café anyway because it was still able to confirm that you are related to a recent recipient of the Green Badge for Military Merit, congratulations."

The waitress never having such an experience before was in shock. She just assumed all computer chips worked unconditionally, and never broke.

After Sue-Anne had her chip scanned, the bill was paid in full and the waitress was now waiting for a tip. This was one of the rare moments cash was still being used. Karl dug into his pocket and realized that he had no change.

"Sue-Anne gave Karl the look, then dug into her own purse for change, and gave what she could to the waitress, who thanked her as she placed the coins in her apron pockets.

"Ok, I will talk to you later. I love you; don't stay in the oxygen tank for too long," Karl warned as he kissed Sue-Anne good bye.

Karl's mother's house was only a couple of blocks away from the restaurant, but he decided to take a taxi-pod, just to be safe.

As he thanked the taxi driver, Karl waved to his mother as he spotted her looking out of the window. The door opened before he had a chance to knock.

"Karl, you won. I just heard on the news, how wonderful."

Karl yelped in pain when his mother gave him hug.

"Karl you look like you were flogged? This is the way your father looked a few days before he disappeared." Mae lifted up Karl's shirt and gasped as she examined the bruises all over his back.

"I was flogged and the gold necklace I bought Sue-Anne is gone and so is my com-corder phone."

"Oh my God, Karl, your back and front are black and blue, and I suppose you will look worse tomorrow. The necklace and phone can be replaced."

"Mom, we have to make an extra effort to enjoy our lives despite our losses. Dad and Danny would have wanted it that way."

"You sure don't look like you are enjoying life to me, you look half dead."

"After our visit I will be heading over to Doctor Gale's office."

"Karl you have to remember all the rules so you can follow them, and avoid all this trouble."

"I know I look bad now, but on New Year's Day I will look great. I will have Sue-Anne on my arm."

"When you do your half a cup full routine, you remind me of how much you are like Danny, but smaller," Mae said trying not to cry. "How could anyone flog someone who looks so frail? If only those Backbencher Kids were forced to show their faces. They hide behind those masks while attacking people who are just minding their own business."

"Well you know what they say about people when their faces are behind masks; they are free to be themselves."

"You have to be a lot more careful. You need to see all these rituals we do under the occupation as a game. Your father took everything to heart, just the way you are doing now. Don't make the same mistakes as your father."

"I am trying not to."

"You look so thin and frail, why would they flog you? Were they trying to kill you?" Mae asked as she directed Karl to her kitchen so she could warm a plate of fried chicken in the microwave.

"They said I swore at Mrs. Stern. You remember Mrs. Stern?"

"How can I not remember her? Whenever I see her downtown, I can't figure out what scares me the most; her or that experimental Flying Spying Gun that is always accompanying her."

"She detained me this morning for not being at my post Monday morning during General Ono's reading of the Manifesto of Truth."

"Isn't she the president of the two Downtown Improvement committees? Why would she be involved?"

"I don't know, she seems to be involved in everything."

"I know you wouldn't swear at anyone. The only way a person could prove their innocence is if the situation had been recorded, and of course that is not allowed. How did she find out that you left your post, and why did they send someone from the two Downtown Improvement Committees in the first place?"

"My house computer reported me missing from my post," Karl explained as he pushed the plate of chicken away. I have no idea what the two Downtown Improvement Committees have to do with anything."

"This used to be your favorite food, Karl. It doesn't look like you are eating enough to keep a bird alive. Your father is dead, now Danny is dead; I need you to stay alive."

"Mom, I said that I was trying my best. I am sure I will put on weight once I am married."

"I certainly hope so. I thought I was going to hear from the panel this month but I heard Doctor Gale was refusing to participate." Mae poured the fortified tea as she spoke. "Give kids like that a bit of power, and there you go, anyone walking down the street could get flogged based on hearsay. They gain their social position through brutality. You are educated Karl, you don't ever have to be brutal to gain power. Remember that for me."

"You know I will Mom."

"Karl I worry about you. Dan always seemed to have the Teflon that you lacked. Once you are hurt, the pain sticks to you like glue; you never seem to let go of it."

"How are you doing, Mom?" Karl asked as he drank his tea.

"I am fine now. I was probably feeling as bad as you are looking until I heard that you won the lottery.

ESCAPE FROM TUT ISLAND

Winning the lottery is great luck. You know how many odds were against you. You can take Sue-Anne to the place of her dreams as a honeymoon present."

"What about the place of my dreams, Mom?"

"I am sure the place of your dreams, will be the place of her dreams too."

After Karl's visit with his mother was over, he walked to his doctor's office. His forehead was automatically scanned as he walked through the door and he was notified that his chip was no longer working.

The young receptionist, startled to see Karl looking so hurt, led him to a room next to Dr. Gale's office.

"Mr. Parks, were you assaulted?" The receptionist asked as she lowered her surgical mask.

Before Karl was able to respond, the receptionist was already taking pictures of his injured face and back.

"We will keep these photographs on file in case you decide to press charges," Karl nodded in agreement.

"I was flogged. The Backbencher Kids flogged me. I need something for the pain. And my chips are broken."

"We will keep these photographs on file in case you decide to press charges," Karl nodded in agreement.

As Karl waited patiently for Dr. Gale he could hear her arguing with someone in her office. "I don't understand why I am being placed under surveillance. As a doctor I take great pride that I happen to see more patients over a hundred years old than any other doctor in District 2021. It is unbelievable that I am being put under investigation just because my patients are living to such an old age."

"Part of the problem, Doctor Gale, is that you do not go to the monthly Panel meetings. Most of the doctors attend these meetings and have no problem aligning their decision making process with General Ono's. We need our doctors to make decisions which fit into our unity by design; whereas your decisions sometimes fall outside the box. Good day Doctor Gale."

Karl realized that there was a lot more going on in the world than he was aware of.

Dr. Gale walked into the room, holding Karl's file, forcing a smile, but her eyes were swollen with hard to fight-back tear drops.

Karl glanced around Doctor Gale's waiting room one last time, to see how many people waiting were actually a hundred years old. He didn't see any. Most of the people didn't look thirty let alone a hundred.

CHAPTER 13:
THE MESSENGER

George struggled to maintain the same pace he used to maintain when he was in his early 20's, and was just beginning his career as a mail carrier. As he aged he found it harder to smile. He had twenty-two black envelopes to deliver, a terrible thing to have to do on Christmas Day. Someone had to deliver the mail. One day they would probably have a robot doing this job, but progress hadn't gotten that far yet.

It was now a capital offense, within the Federation's jurisdiction, to kill a mail carrier. Botmen were authorized to shoot on sight, anyone who tried to harm a mail carrier.

George always carried a gun to defend himself against hostiles. He had his com-corder phone with him at all times. He also carried an alarm to break the silence whenever he felt hat he was in danger.

Even though mail carriers had more ways to protect themselves, than ever before, George felt a despair that only a dose of artificial joy could cure.

The emptiness George felt was sometimes unbearable and he was always grateful that the Receptor Bloc Compound responded as quickly as it did when he swallowed two of the tiny white pills, four times a day.

As the Receptor Bloc Compound eased George's emptiness, he began to lose himself in memories of the good old days.

There was a time, a long time ago, when George was still a young man, mail carriers were welcomed by all and that was why George, as a boy, wanted to become a mail carrier. He lost himself in memories of delivering holiday greeting cards to happier people. He remembered when he was invited into people's homes for hot chocolate, on a cold snowy day. Those were the days when everyone said hello to him as he worked his route, delivering mail. Those were different and gentler times in a kinder world.

In the old days, before the occupation, no one expected a death sentence if insolvency occurred, especially not on Christmas Day. It was just assumed that creditors could not physically harm debtors. George never imagined that one-day he would be delivering a death sentence. If George had been able to foresee this change in events, he may have chosen a different line of work.

George listened to the words coming from the loud speakers scattered along the street.

"After we bring on the End, the Beginning is our promised time of eternal peace and happiness. We must continue to believe in this promise. As long as we are strong in our faith that the beginning will come, we will be strong enough to fight until the end. We are never alone. General Ono sees each and every one of you, not just as electronic specs, but as Unity."

George regretted not having children until he saw how vicious many of his friends' children were toward their own parents. During the time the Minese were undergoing the occupation of Tut Island and renaming the Island, District 2021, families were torn and children turned against their own parents.

Even though it was a fact of life under General Ono's rule, that anyone with working chips could be traced, if necessary; such knowledge did not comfort George. Knowing that every movement could be traced contributed to George's feeling of alienation.

ESCAPE FROM TUT ISLAND

As George delivered the mail he spoke to no one and no one spoke to him.

George could feel the Receptor Bloc Compound beginning to numb his brain. He no longer felt the sadness that was still so visible on his face.

George tried to listen to the Manifesto of Truth readings as they were being transmitted through the familiar speakers lining the streets, but his own words echoing in his mind, got in the way.

"The Ending needs everyone to be productive because without the Ending there can be no Beginning," George realized that no one, not even an old man should remain idle. George continued delivering the mail and would continue until the day he died. No one retired any more. After losing the last war, the struggle to pay off the debt would continue for generations to come.

George knocked on the brown oak door, at 277 Valleyview Rd. He glanced at the black envelope for a moment and he wished that he could make it disappear. Of course tampering with the mail was a capital offense, especially for mail carriers.

As George ignored his own wishes he handed Gloria Gibson the black envelope while scanning her forehead. He felt for her, but he was only doing his job. George heard a faint scream echoing down the street as he left the building as fast as he could. George continued to do his work, even though he would not describe it as good work, nevertheless it was a job.

Gloria threw the envelope on the floor and stared at the black file in disbelief.

The letter declared that their home must be sold at the end of the month and their creditors would be paid the money they were owed from the proceeds of the sell. A copy of this statement had been filed with the Ministry of Files.

The bailiffs would be arriving in ten days to change the locks on their doors, and after that they would be taken away to be recycled into winners. Their status would be documented in the Detachment's Database and the information would be available to all in the occupied world to see.

Gloria's panic overpowered her mind. The next Recycling Day was in twenty-eight days and the notice suggested that she should prepare herself and her family to be recycled. She did not know how to prepare. Gloria cried.

Now, there were only twenty-one black files left in George's mail bag.

George glanced at his wristwatch and realized he had two minutes to go before he could stop and take a lunch break. He waited patiently for two minutes until Control Center gave him the signal that his morning shift was now complete. He decided that he would have lunch at the Golden Leaf Café. It was one of the most popular cafés in town and he enjoyed going there. He placed his head on the door scanner and waited patiently. Once his forehead was scanned he was allowed to enter the Café.

As Karl and Sue-Anne were leaving the restaurant, George waved and smiled, forcing them to wave and smile back.

Sue-Anne and Karl didn't really hate George; they only felt contempt for him, for everyone hated mail carriers.

George waved to people whenever he could for the waves made him feel that he was still part of a community, and the people around him were still his neighbors. The waves also make him feel less hated. The more he waved, the more he looked like a fool.

George didn't like the Recycling Days any more than anyone else did, especially this one which fell on Christmas Eve. These were days of sacrifice. The debt had to be paid somehow.

ESCAPE FROM TUT ISLAND

George sat at his favorite table and placed the headphones on his head so that he could listen to General Ono's morning speech again. Although not compulsory, citizens often felt more assured that they were well informed after listening to General Ono's recordings repeatedly.

George logged into the dietary channel. George accepted the computer generated suggestion. George listened to re-runs of General Ono reading the Manifesto of Truth.

"The Ending is not a war. The Ending is the way the Federation of Unity prevents war. If individuals did not suffer the full consequences of their insolvency, then the Federation would have fewer resources to fight until the end. Today, life is no longer a right. Life is a privilege only reserved for General Ono to decide who has earned their right to life. This is the law of the Moral Authority and this law must be obeyed." General Ono continued to read from his script.

After eating his Christmas Day lunch consisting of an extra strength wafer and bottled water, George left the café and continued to deliver the mail.

CHAPTER 14:
DISCOVERY

Gloria Gibson was outraged that she and her children had become victim of Mark's failure to be a good provider, especially on Christmas Day. Gloria dialed her husband's phone number. He sounded irritated that his relaxing drink with the neighbor next door had been interrupted.

Mark knew the black file would be arriving any day. He had no idea what he could say to make it better. Mark did nothing to prepare Gloria for the shock. Mark never discussed difficult subjects about the outside world with Gloria, for it would be rude to do so. He preferred avoiding discussions with her most of the time. She was never concerned about what went on outside the home, and Mark usually preferred it that way.

The hardness of the outside world contrasted too harshly with Gloria's conditioned fragility. Mark always tried to protect his wife. He realized that he had failed in his duty as a man, as a husband and as a father. Gloria screamed as she waved the black file in front of the screen. The reality of insolvency had reached the Gibson family. They were now dispossessed.

Mark tried to calm Gloria.

"What are we going to do?" Gloria asked frantically, hoping Mark would have a solution.

"We can do nothing," Mark replied.

"I suppose nothing is the only thing you have been good at doing," Gloria scoffed.

ESCAPE FROM TUT ISLAND

"I meant that there is nothing we can do now, our fate is sealed. We will have to survive in shelters until our allowed time is used up, then we will have to hope things will turn out all right," Mark added.

"And what about our boys, how will they cope when taken away to a government institution?" Gloria knew, without a home, or a way to make ends meet, the children would be taken away from them by the Ministry of Child Protection."

Gloria felt the rage building inside her. Mark had failed to provide for his family, and now she was paying the price for marrying the wrong man.

"Is that it, Mark? Is that your plan? We are going to hope that things will turn out all right? We will have to put everything we are allowed to keep in a grocery cart, and push it around until we are noticed by someone from one of the Downtown Improvement Committees. It will only be a matter of time before the Backbencher Kids lock us in a cage, and we will be left in there, fed by strangers until next month's Recycling Day arrives?" Gloria was furious with Mark and hung the phone up before Mark could apologize.

Gloria wished she had listened to her Mother's warnings about Mark years ago. Both her parents died over a decade ago. Mark and her children are the only family she had left. Her father, like many men, died at an early age. Her mother had asked for the Mercy a few days after her father's funeral.

Gloria used to believe in the greatness of the Federation of Unity and the glorious future that was being promised. She once welcomed the Central Bank of Mina's rising power and domination. Today she hated General Ono and his army of occupiers, she hated Mark and she hated herself.

Gloria glared at the familiar picture of the Golden Scales on her wall. It had been hanging there for many years. And today she hated that picture more than ever before. She grabbed it from the wall and threw it on the floor and stomped on it until it was broken into so many pieces, it couldn't be broken any further.

Gloria felt betrayed. Mark had lied to her. The Golden Scales had failed her, and the promise of the fine balance was never meant to be.

When Mark returned home, around 11 PM, Gloria was waiting for him. It was quick and painless. Gloria aimed for the heart and Mark died instantly. Then Gloria phoned 911, and then shot herself.

As the sound of gun shots awoke the children, Billy and Joey ran into their parents' bedroom finding both parents' blood pouring out from their gunshot wounds. Billy and Joey were in shock as they sat on the floor and cried hysterically.

Mark and Gloria had reached their Ending. They were now detached from life, as one knows life to be. We must now forget about them. The boys' lives would be changed forever.

CHAPTER 15:
RESPONSE

Constable James Bell awoke with a start. He had fallen asleep at his desk. And as he awoke with a jolt, the Christmas tree on the desk had fallen over.

The nights were usually quiet now, since the issuing of the black files, most of the members of the Detachment fell asleep waiting for calls to wake them up.

A deep voice spoke to him from a small two way radio clipped to his uniform jacket. A murder suicide had been reported. The victims would be dead on arrival. Two boys would need to be processed by Child Protection.

James bought another cup of hot coffee from the vending machine and prepared himself for his duties. He opened an issue pack 'Receptor Bloc Compound pills and administered his dose, to enhance his detachment.

As James threw the wrapper into the waste paper basket, an automated voice thanked him for doing his part in keeping the office clean. A lottery ticket popped out from the side of the basket. He added it to the pile of tickets in his desk drawer.

James never checked his tickets. He didn't believe he could ever win.

James climbed into his police car and flew to the Gibson residence. He parked beside the ambulance already parked on the rooftop. Attendants placed each body on a stretcher and carried them away.

James entered the gruesome scene at 1412 Centralized Park Ave. and performed his duties with clinical professionalism. He had been a member of the Detachment for twelve years and his tasks were well practiced.

There were all kinds of variations of murder suicides during the week when Black Files were issued. Most of these murder-suicides were predictable. Gloria and Mark's murder-suicide was no different. James made a note so it could be added to his report that a black file addressed to Mark was found in Gloria's purse at the scene.

James Bell phoned the Ministry of Child Protection. Soon the boys would be taken to their new home.

The Ministry of Child Protection had been built on an island and it was only accessible by boat and jeep. Most of the children were monitored so closely that any hope of escape and magically returning to their old lives was a short lived fantasy.

Billy and Joey would be protected and educated until they reached the age of nineteen. Billy was thirteen and Joey was fifteen.

Mary Brown arrived from Child Protection.

As James Bell returned to his office, he found it difficult to remember the details of the incident. The incident was resolved so now he must move on. He plugged his watch into the computer so that he could transfer his notes to the House of Detachment's database. After finishing his report James changed his mood by taking an extra dose of Receptor Bloc Compound. He threw the wrapper away. A lottery ticket popped out from the side of the basket. He automatically retrieved the lottery ticket and threw it into his desk drawer. James fell into a dreamless sleep.

CHAPTER 16:
CHANGE OF LIFE

The boys sat in the back seat of the car. Joey told his younger brother that everything was going to work out fine. Billy looked outside the window and hoped his brother was right but felt doubtful.

Mary Brown parked the car and led the boys to the classification department for processing. This building was linked to the Detachment's command post.

The Ministry of Child Protection protected children through environmental design. The main building served as school and dining hall but the most important function was its role in security management as a command post which was why it was surrounded by small cottages. Many experiments were conducted at this complex.

This island had no trees, bushes or rocks again by design. The boys would have nowhere to hide should they decide to escape. The buildings had many windows. The perimeter lights illuminated the grounds, which were visible from any point within the main building.

As Billy and Joey were escorted down the hall, they could see the house parent scanning the tidy rows of monitors as surveillance cameras were feeding continual images of sleeping boys into them.

The boys were quickly processed and were told to take showers after they had their I.D. chips scanned to verify that the new information had been properly updated. The surveillance cameras watched the boys, as they stood naked in the huge shower stall. They were issued bags for their old clothes. Their old clothes would be thrown away but must be documented first.

Then the boys were issued cadet military styled uniforms that were worn by all the children living under the Ministry of Child Protection. Soon they would be receiving gold name plates to be pinned to their shirts. In the meantime, the boys would wear temporary name tags. Billy and Joey didn't care. They hated their new dwelling and knew it would never be home. They wanted to return to their old home and the life they used to have.

The boys were separated. Jane Harris was the house parent on duty. She gave Billy a chocolate Receptor Bloc Compound, which immediately calmed him. Actually calling the Receptor Bloc's effect 'calming' was an understatement. Billy began to feel numb. Soon, he was sleeping in the cottage designated for boys his own age, while someone he used to be, deep inside was beginning to die.

Joey was taken to another cottage, which housed older boys, and he too was issued a bed and a Receptor Bloc Compound. Joey didn't sleep. He lay awake in bed feeling his rage growing inside him. He wondered how his life could have changed so drastically without an explanation. He blamed his mother and hated her for betraying him in such a sudden and cruel way on Christmas Day.

CHAPTER 17:
WHERE IS THE BATTLE?

On the other side of the earth, in the Kingdom of Belunga, a battle was raging. Kneeling on the scorched earth, a young man wearing camouflage, aimed his anti-aircraft gun at the unmanned aircraft over head. The carbon-graphite composite aircraft needed neither cockpit nor windows. Jacob Coaltonstone, its pilot, sat safely thousands of miles away at his station situated in the west wing of the Coalton Base, on Tut Island, officially referred to as District 2021. Hundreds of similar aircraft were bombing targets nearby.

The young man wearing camouflage felt the ground shake underneath his boots which were too big. The unmanned aircraft roared in the sky above.

The young man, wearing camouflage, knew the importance of his mission. If he succeeded in shooting down the aircraft he would become a hero and his people would learn more about the mighty enemy's technology. If he succeeded in accomplishing his mission, there would be one less aircraft bombing his people. The young man wearing camouflage hoped he could win this battle and return to his wives.

The young man, wearing camouflage, locked the surface-to-air missile launcher onto the unmanned aerial vehicle. A red light and a deafening alarm alerted Jacob Coaltonstone who was piloting the aerial vehicle thousands of miles away, in Coalton.

Jacob Coaltonstone was thankful that he was fighting for the winning side. This was Jacob's first job working for the Ministry of Aerial Defense. Jacob wore the white uniform worn by the officers that were in his position. He pushed the red button on the joystick beside his computer console. A bomb from the aerial vehicle was launched. The young man wearing the camouflage outfit on the other side of the earth, in the Kingdom of Belunga, was blown to bits and died instantly.

Jacob watched as his target exploded in living color, to the cheers of the many young men and women sitting at nearby war stations situated at the base in Coalton.

The Battle had been won. It would soon be time to eat Christmas dinner together as a team.

Jacob basked in the glory of the moment and waved his arms in the air. He ran around the room so that his comrades could slap his palms with their sweaty hands. They shared the joy of their friend's victory and certain glory.

Another young man, wearing camouflage on the other side of the world in the land of Belunga, would soon be the next loser.

The unmanned aircraft was filming the battle as it progressed. Every single detail of this conflict in Belunga was transmitted to Jacob's battle station located in the semi-secret bunker, twelve hundred feet underground. This war video would be played most likely after General Ono's reading from the Manifesto of Truth, several times during the next few days, transforming Jacob Coaltonstone into an instant war hero soon to be distinguished as a man of military merit.

To be a war hero during these times of conflict would mean that Jacob would be issued a Medal of Honor. The medal would be attached to his uniform elevating him in rank and giving him a raise in pay. There would be even more eager salutes as he walked by. He savored the moment and looked forward to his bright future.

Jacob would be repeating this story many times to his children and their children. He tried to memorize every detail as he watched the battle replay on his computer. Jacob might even be asked to pose for a recruiting poster.

No doubt he would be wearing his new medal at his cousin's wedding, on New Year's Day.

On the other side of the world, in the Kingdom of Beluga, a group of young men, wearing camouflage uniforms, arrived to remove the remains of the previous young man who was wearing camouflage. The young men try to find every part of him they can.

A new replacement arrived to replace another young man who was just killed in the land of Belunga.

Overhead, thousands of unmanned aerial vehicles increased their elevation.

The bombs continued to fall.

The sky was on fire.

CHAPTER 18:
ANOTHER SHOCK

"What is that thing doing in our room?" Betty screamed.

"Allan, wake up!" Betty shouted at Allan, as she glared at IQ who was still standing over their bed. Betty shook Allan with all her might, accidentally pushing him out of their bed onto the hard floor.

IQ rushed to Allan's aid. Medical instruments quickly appeared from his chest. Allan lay wide eyed on the floor while staring at IQ in disbelief. IQ was about to put a stethoscope on Allan's heart so that he could assess Allan's heart health. "Sir, your heart is beating over the recommended rate for a man your age. The test IQ performed activated a printout; a monogram of Allan's heart beat spouted out from IQ's mouth and landed on Allan's stomach.

IQ was about to check Betty's heartbeat until Allan protested.

"Stop you idiot" Allan yelled at IQ as he swung his hand in between IQ and his wife. Allan felt his hand ache as if he had hit a piece of metal.

"I woke up with that thing staring at me. It must have been staring at me while I was sleeping. It is still staring at me," Betty complained as her eyes swelled with tears.

"Betty I am so sorry," Allan replied while Betty choked back tears.

"Allan why is that thing in our room? Isn't it bad enough that our Christmas has been ruined?" Betty asked.

"What the hell are you doing in our room?" Allan asked IQ.

"I thought I told you to stay in the hallway," Allan said blaming himself for this terrible introduction to IQ.

"I am programmed to protect you when you are at your most vulnerable, Sir," IQ explained.

"Well you are taking your instructions a little too literally," Allan said trying not to shout.

"I heard strange noises coming from your room, and when I entered, I noticed you both had your eyes closed. You were in a state where both of you were lacking consciousness. I was protecting you the way I am programmed to do."

Allan and Betty stared at IQ in disbelief.

"Weren't you programmed to tell the difference between the sleeping and the dead? Can't you just guard our door within the parameters of common sense and decency?" Allan asked. "I mean our room is private and you are scaring my wife."

"I am going to call Daddy," Betty jumped out of bed and began inputting her father's number into her com-corder phone.

"I don't want that thing in the house staring at me while I am sleeping."

"It is very early; I don't think you should wake him. I will ask the programmers to reprogram IQ so that he stays out of our bedroom unless he is actually called or if there is an emergency. Allan was afraid of Betty's father because he had such a bad temper.

"I don't want that thing in the house," Betty said again as she waited impatiently for her father to answer the com-corder phone.

"I am not a thing," protested IQ. "I am self-aware which makes me a legal life form. And in many ways I am more efficient than you are. I don't wait for emergencies to happen before I act. I am programmed to act in order to prevent emergencies."

IQ opened a compartment door revealing the screen in his abdomen.

"Would you like to see the odds which are against your species surviving this millennium?"

"No, I would not," Allan said. "I have to work tomorrow morning and I want to get some shut eye."

IQ closed his terminal screen.

"Why isn't Daddy answering? It is bad enough that you didn't come home until three o'clock in the morning, without telling me why. I really did think you were having an affair. I was worrying about it for hours. But no woman would feel like making love while that thing was watching or even nearby." Betty began to cry, as she dialed her father's number a second time. "Why did you bring that thing into our house, without asking me first?"

The com-corder phone rang eight times before her father answered.

"Daddy, I don't want that thing in our house," Betty screamed over the com-corder phone as she pointed to IQ.

"Dear, please, calm down, I was sound asleep when you called."

"Daddy, I woke up to that thing staring at me. Why is it in our house? Can't you make it go away? It gave me such a fright; I almost had a heart attack. It must have been staring at me while I was sleeping, possibly for hours. I will let you speak to Allan. He doesn't want that thing in our house either," Betty said as she moved over to let Allan sole access to the com-corder phone.

"Speak to Daddy; tell him we don't want that thing in our house," Betty told Allan.

"Good morning Sir, I am sorry to disturb you so early in the morning. I know you must have been sleeping. Betty is very upset," Allan said apologetically.

"Is this an emergency? Why is Betty so upset? Is she ill? Are the children ill?"

Betty pushed Allan a little so her face could be seen in the monitor.

"Daddy, I want to know why Allan didn't get home until three in the morning, why did he miss Christmas dinner and why do we have that thing in our house?" Betty pointed the cam-corder phone straight at IQ. If the phone had been a gun, IQ would have not been left standing.

"Excuse me," IQ said as he moved in front of the monitor so that his face could be shown on the terminal.

"Sir, I resent being called a thing, I am self-aware, and therefore I am legally a life form. I was doing my duty by watching over my partner and his wife while they were at their most vulnerable. We are under red alert Sir, and there is a lot of background information which is classified that the wife should not hear, which validates my behavior, Sir."

"Daddy, I don't want to be called 'the wife' by that thing and I don't want to be sleeping with that thing watching me, please do something," Betty started to cry again as she pushed IQ out of the way.

Allan's two little girls, both dressed in pink pajamas, rushed into the room carrying their blankets; half asleep but still curious, wondering what the commotion was all about.

"What is that? Is that another Christmas present?" Susan the youngest girl asked, as she pointed to IQ.

"I think that is your Daddy's new partner," Betty whispered to the girls without even glancing at IQ.

"He is funny looking," Susan said as she walked over to IQ and examined him carefully, and then placed her finger into his nostril.

"What do you do?" Brenda asked IQ as she watched Susan interacting with IQ.

"Your finger is in my nostril and this is a complete violation of my personal parameters," IQ said in protest.

"I am sorry," Susan said unconvincingly since she was giggling way too hard to be truly sorry.

"What do you do?" Brenda asked again.

"I am primarily programmed to analyze information, and to calculate the probability of an expected or more correctly, a desired outcome.

I have all the current world maps in my database, which are updated as we succeed in our quest for global domination and expansion. My database holds information equivalent to a medical doctor and a military engineer. I can perform emergency surgery and I can also build bridges. I am programmed with the skills equivalent to a black belt in karate. I have the added advantage of having laser beams in my grippers, which can cut through diamonds and destroy asteroids.

IQ opened the compartment which revealed the screen which was being stored in his abdomen.

"Would you like to see the odds which are against your species surviving this millennium?

The girls started to giggle uncontrollably again.

"Do we own you?" Brenda asked.

"I am actually the property of the Ministry of Defense but I am being loaned out to the two Downtown Improvement Committees so I can be your Daddy's partner," IQ said as he lured the child's finger out of his nose.

"Much better" he said as the children giggled.

"Do you think you could fix my Ebike? It broke yesterday and Mommy said that Daddy never has time to fix anything," Brenda asked.

"I thought you were working for the Ministry of Transformation? Why do the Downtown Improvement Committees need that thing? Betty asked as she pointed accusingly to IQ.

ESCAPE FROM TUT ISLAND

"Betty, I don't know what Ministry I am working for anymore, but I was given a nice Christmas Bonus maybe we could go out for a movie and dinner after; just the two of us."

The girls rushed to the monitor when they saw that their grandfather was still on line even though their parents were ignoring him and talking to each other.

"Hi Grandpa, Merry Christmas," both girls said in unison.

"Hello girls, how would you like to fly through the heavens and visit the moon for your Christmas vacation? The moon could be your home for two weeks. It will be a lovely escape during the holiday season. The lights on Earth will be beautiful when seen from the heavens. This will be a great opportunity for you girls to visit a heavenly body and call it home. What do you say Betty. You could take a look at the water rock mining project. We own 30% interest in the project so you girls should enjoy that too. This part of the earth can be so unbearably cold in January."

"Daddy, that would be wonderful," Betty said suddenly feeling much better. I would love to fly through the heavens and forget about earthly matters for a couple of weeks," Betty added.

"Sir, I must object," IQ said boldly.

"You object to all my girls going on vacation?"

"No sir. I object to the fact that Earth is not being described as a heavenly body. Earth is clearly part of the heavens too, Sir."

"Of course you are right IQ. Betty, why don't you put the girls back into bed, and I will have a private talk with your husband and his new partner."

"Girls, you need to go to bed now. Thank your grandfather for being such a great grandpa," Betty instructed as she led the girls back to their bedroom.

"Thank you Grandpa," the girls said in unison.

"You are welcome girls. Now let us all get back to bed before it is time for us to wake up," Betty's father said and then hung up.

"Hi Grandpa, Merry Christmas," both girls said in unison.

"Hello girls, how would you like to fly through the heavens and visit the moon for your Christmas vacation? The moon could be your home for two weeks. It will be a lovely escape during the holiday season. The lights on Earth will be beautiful when seen from the heavens. This will be a great opportunity for you girls to visit a heavenly body and call it home. What do you say Betty. You could take a look at the water rock mining project. We own 30% interest in the project so you girls should enjoy that too. This part of the earth can be so unbearably cold in January."

"Daddy, that would be wonderful," Betty said suddenly feeling much better. I would love to fly through the heavens and forget about earthly matters for a couple of weeks," Betty added.

"Sir, I must object," IQ said boldly.

"You object to all my girls going on vacation?"

"No sir. I object to the fact that Earth is not being described as a heavenly body. Earth is clearly part of the heavens too, Sir."

"Of course you are right IQ. Betty, why don't you put the girls back into bed, and I will have a private talk with your husband and his new partner."

"Girls, you need to go to bed now. Thank your grandfather for being such a great grandpa," Betty instructed as she led the girls back to their bedroom.

"Thank you Grandpa," the girls said in unison.

"You are welcome girls. Now let us all get back to bed before it is time for us to wake up," Betty's father said and then hung up.

CHAPTER 19:
THE GUARD

It was early Thursday morning for Allan and Betty. It was almost time for the reading from the Manifesto of Truth again.

IQ made himself comfortable in the hallway.

Betty crawled under the sheets and cuddled up beside Allan. "What did Daddy say last night, after I left the room?"

"Your father said that he is going to make arrangements for your Christmas vacation. IQ is going to be my partner for a while. He may have been taking his preprogrammed commands a little too literally. He is not that bad. He had been programmed to be sensitive and he was only trying to guard us to the best of his ability. He was only assembled a few months ago and it will take time for him to refine his social skills."

"I am so glad that thing is out of our bedroom."

"Me too, your father said that he was going to enroll IQ into an etiquette class. IQ will be working on etiquette while I am having lunch. You could probably help him if you addressed him in a dignified manner. He would like to be called IQ and he promised to only enter our room when we call him, or during an emergency."

"I don't want to live with that thing; I don't want it near the children. Couldn't Daddy find a way to leave it at your office? Why didn't they give you a human partner?

Human partners go home to their own families in the evenings.

"I agree. It is a total invasion of our private space. But I cannot argue with your father, Betty, you try," Allan said. How could anyone be happy being guarded by a bot who might be spying on them? Allan didn't believe that IQ could ever be his real partner. IQ couldn't be trusted; he was just a machine, programmed by the occupiers.

Allan wished that he didn't have to spell out the situation to Betty. He wished that he could share how he really felt, but he couldn't. He couldn't place Betty in danger. He wanted the best for his family. And even if he could tell Betty, how could he explain that IQ was his guard and not his partner? He had no choice. It was her father who got him this job, which led to having a botguard standing on the other side of their bedroom door.

If Betty thought that she was feeling bad, she had no idea how bad Allan was really feeling. He hated his job. He hated processing people as if they were spare car parts. He hated all the secrecy; he didn't even know what Betty's father really did, or why he was wearing his suit and mask so early in the morning.

"I don't know why I don't have a human partner," was all Allan could say. He knew perfectly well that a robot would only betray him when necessary; whereas an ego driven human partner could choose to betray his confidence whenever it benefitted him or his ego to do so.

"Let's go back to sleep. I have to be at work in a couple of hours. I hope you don't mind going to the moon with the kids without me. Your father needs me to stay here and help him do some work with the two Downtown Improvement Committees."

"I don't get why you are working with the Downtown Improvement Committees. What kind of work do they need you to do?"

"I am not sure. It is all very confusing and classified."

"You know I need you too, Allan," Betty said not even trying to hide her disappointment.

Betty understood that her father had ordered this vacation for his convenience.

"Why does Daddy make so many decisions without asking me?" Betty didn't expect an answer.

"Well we are very busy working on a major project with the Downtown Improvement Committees, like I said. You know Mrs. Stern, she is involved," Allan explained.

"Daddy is working with Mrs. Stern and the Downtown Improvement Committees? What is Daddy doing to improve downtown? Is he going to lift the dress code so we can shop for different outfits? That sure would be an improvement. All the clothes stores look the same cause they are selling the same outfits. I thought Daddy didn't like Mrs. Stern and avoided all the parties that she invites him to.

"I know. The whole thing is classified and I really doubt that it has anything to do with changing the dress code," Allan responded.

A teardrop fell from Betty's eye and she didn't say a word. She closed her eyes and pretended that she was sleeping.

Allan closed his eyes and pretended to be asleep too while IQ was trying to figure out why humans behaved so strangely.

CHAPTER 20:
1ST DAY AT MINISTRY OF PROTECTION

As Joey awoke he realized that he did not have a horrible dream. His life really was a nightmare now, and the only way out would be death or a miracle. He looked around and saw a row of sleepy boys his own age wearing identical pajamas labeled with each boy's name, serial number and aging-out date.

Jane Harris entered the room and told the boys to be more efficient. Lying in bed was not an option. The boys who were scheduled to shower were hurried into the shower stalls.

As the boys formed a line in the dining room, Joey could see his brother and waved to him. Billy waved back.

As the boys were given their rations of extra strength wafers and bottled water they were signaled to march to their designated seats in the cafeteria in order of aging out date.

Joey fought back tears as he wondered how he would survive living like this for another two years. Once he aging out from this place he wondered what would happen to his little brother.

The boy sitting next to Joey asked if he wanted his wafer.

"I don't really like it but I am hungry so I need to eat something," Joey replied as he realized that the boy just ignored what he had just said and grabbed his wafer anyway.

"Hey give me back my food," Joey demanded as the he tried to grab the wafer back. The boy threw his water at him and they began to fight violently. Tables were turned over; other boys scrambled to get out of the way. Flying wafers were quickly gathered by the bigger boys, and hoarded.

Jane Harris blew her whistle frantically and quickly removed her Beam Pen that was stored in a holder on her utility belt, and aimed it into the boys' eyes. She triggered the switch to the on position. The bright laser beam obscured the boys' vision, causing confusion and temporary blindness.

The boys were fighting with each other so violently that Jane Harris missed her target. She triggered another switch on the Beam Pen sending a radar signal to the children's' brains producing a deafening sound while creating even more confusion. The boys were temporarily stunned. Security staff marched into the dining room and led the two boys away to be fitted with Stun Belts.

Billy cried as his brother was taken away. His house parent gave him an extra dose of Receptor Bloc Compound to soothe him.

"He started it," Joey said, as he pointed to the other boy. He tried to steal my wafer from me."

"I did not. You attacked me for no reason."

"I don't want to hear a word from either one of you and I certainly hope that you will be reflecting on how this coming new year will either make or break both of you," John Davis said as he marched the boys to the security officer. The officer would be in charge of placing the Stun Belts under the boys' clothes. The Stun Belts would be locked into place for an indefinite period of time.

The Beam Pens were only meant to control children with mild behavior problems. In time these children would learn to respond to instructions appropriately and would soon never talk back to authority. These boys appeared to have a violent streak in them, which would make them very difficult to control especially when the housing complex was so understaffed.

Once the Stun Belt was in place, the house parent could send the child a jolt of electricity strong enough to force him to his knees if necessary, especially when the child was deemed to be aggressive. These remote control devices seemed to be all that was needed to keep a young person's passions under control and to protect him and others from his natural tendency to become violent when feeling trapped.

The Ministry of Child Protection often tested state of the art technology during their child management endeavors.

CHAPTER 21:
THE VICTOR'S JUSTICE

It was Thursday morning and time for the reading from the Manifesto of Truth. Karl struggled to get out of his bed. His body hurt more today than it did yesterday. Christmas Day was just another day lost in time.

Karl felt a force pushing him backwards. He tried to fight back but he couldn't. The force was stronger than he was.

Karl could hear a voice and it sounded like Danny's.

"Karl can you feel me? I am inside you."

"Danny?" Karl asked feeling like he had actually gone mad.

"Can you hear me?" Danny asked Karl.

"You won't believe what I have been through. You wouldn't believe what kind of chaos there was at the end. They didn't let me through the Gate. The guard at the Gate pushed me away."

"I find that hard to believe, I must be imagining this."

"No, you are not imagining anything. It is me. You can't let me die."

"You are dead. I have a copy of your certificate of military merit hanging on the wall. You died a hero. Why wouldn't they let you through the Gate?"

"Well, the guard at the Gate didn't give me a reason. Lots of people were let in, but not me. My spirit needs a home. When I died, I felt incredible pain. I was blown to bits and it really hurt. There was a tunnel of light inside an endless space of darkness. The heat was unbearable. And then I was caught up in this furious wind. And finally I found myself in you. I felt myself being pulled by this irresistible force, I could hear it ticking.

"You mean my heart, pulled you in? That is totally unbelievable.'

"Karl, the fighting was awful. It was hard to know what side I was actually on. The fighting was barbaric. It was like what I said before. I became nothing so quickly," Danny explained to Karl.

Karl tried to speak, but he didn't know what to say. He found it hard to believe that he was not imagining all of this.

"What is new with you Karl?"

"I suppose you know I am getting married to Sue-Anne on New Year's Day.'

"If I were alive, and had a reasonable chance for a future, she would have married me, you know," Danny grumbled.

"Who cares about what might have been? We could go on about 'what might have been' forever. I love Sue-Anne, and Sue-Anne loves me and you are dead."

"Of course Sue-Anne loves you, now, because you look so much like me."

"Let's change the subject."

"Ok. Why are you putting our body at risk?"

"Our body?"

"Why get involved with the power struggle between the dispossessed and General Ono's power brokers. It is a battle that can't be won. It might as well be legislated poverty; the gap between the haves and have nots is impossible to close. Nowadays social mobility is just a dream," Danny argued.

"Yes, mobility is especially difficult when you are missing all your body parts."

"So, why did you really make that video, it could get us killed?" Danny asked.

"I took the video by accident. I was hanging on to it because I believed it showed the crimes against humanity. My God these power brokers don't even have to show their face, let alone their nametags when they are brutalizing near starving people."

"I know your intentions are good, but you are very naïve, bro. No one cares about rights of man, unless it is them that have lost those rights. Everyone else takes the rights of man for granted."

"I actually lost my phone. I don't know what is going to happen to me now."

"You mean us."

"No, I mean me."

"Well, you should have left the whole thing alone. You can't do anything to change anything. Dying for a principle is stupid."

"Well what did you die for?"

"I don't know. I was just in the wrong place at the wrong time, and this strange weapon was chasing me and took over my impulses so I couldn't fight back. I assumed that I would die fighting, I had no idea I was going to die like that."

"Isn't that what makes a man great, that he is willing to die for his principles not just by accident?"

"What does it matter what a person dies for? No one will know in the end."

"No one should be recycled just because they owe money. Most of those debts have been unfairly inflated. The Central Bank of Mina keep charging fees for not having sufficient funds and landlords keep putting rents up as their properties decay. Some of my clients have had a broken toilet for six years. Employers refuse to pay a livable wage even to those who went into personal debt so they could enter a profession. The price paid for being poor shouldn't be a person's body parts."

Before Danny could reply in agreement there was a firm knock at the door.

"You better get the door," Danny said.

"You still talk to me as if I need every little thing explained to me," Karl complained.

As Karl opened the door, his heart missed sank as it did whenever he saw Mrs. Stern at his door. She was standing holding her toy dog in one arm and waving his phone with her free hand, while her Flying Spying Gun was on guard by her side in its usual way.

"Hello, Karl, we are meeting once again, isn't that precious," Mrs. Stern walked in as she owned Karl's apartment. "My colleagues informed me that they found this com-corder phone on the sidewalk, and we traced it to you. Please kneel," Mrs. Stern from the Ministry of Vagrancy and the Downtown Improvement Committees demanded as Teacup sniffed around to find a place to pee.

"Yes, Ma'am," Karl said as he responded obediently.

"Besides the good news that we found your com-corder phone and are returning it to you; we have transferred your name from the Botman regiment 'D' list to the Botman regiment 'A' list. We have updated your new chips which Doctor Gale installed for you, yesterday. Your knowledge of mathematics and electronics is very impressive and is one of many indications that you will make a fine fit for our Botman program. Good day Karl," Mrs. Stern said as she patted Karl's head which triggered Teacup to bark wildly until he too was patted on the head.

"Good day Karl."

"Ma'am did you find a rectangular box all wrapped up? It would have looked like a Christmas present and might have been lying on the ground next to my phone."

"No, I didn't Karl."

"Good day Ma'am."

"Check your com-corder phone," Danny insisted.

"I am too scared," Karl replied.

"You are on now the Botman 'A' list; your middle name should be fearless not fear, bro."

Danny refused to take no for an answer, not because he didn't respect Karl's personal parameters, but because the suspense was killing him.

"My God, my whole com-corder phone has been erased back to its default state."

"Well it is lucky they didn't erase you. It is bad enough that they put you on the Botman regiment 'A' list. You will be the wimpiest Botman in the regiment's history. You will always be compared to me, so you better start getting used to it. What kind of gun was that flying by Mrs. Stern's side? It looks exactly like the weapon that chased me before it killed me."

"Are you sure?"

"Of course I am sure."

"It is called a Flying Spying Gun. They are only supposed to be in the experimental stage according to what I was reading about them on the internet."

"What stops someone from taking one of those guns remotely and using it to attack someone while they remain invisible?"

"I don't know. Are you sure that is what killed you when you were fighting in Belunga?"

"I wasn't fighting in the end, I was running. Of course I am sure. I couldn't fight it. It was like it had control over my body. My impulses were being controlled. I was blown up while running from it. I was running like a coward. I couldn't even fight it like a man."

"Danny you died a hero. You made me a relative of a warrior who was awarded a certificate the Green Badge for Military Merit."

"I know what happened. I could see it in my helmet mirror as it was chasing me."

"Those spying flying guns are very experimental. The Eel technology is rather unpredictable."

"I know that is what killed me. And the finality of death means everything we know as men, no longer exists for us. Why risk your life to show the truth about the human condition when you have Sue-Anne to live for?

"I told you the video was made by mistake. All I know is that I will make a lousy Botman."

"Yes, but you kept that video at our peril to do what; to educate the public about the rights of man. All they will do is laugh at your naiveté. Having such a video on your phone has now lowered our quality of life by giving that Mrs. Stern and whoever she is working for an excuse to intrude and interfere in our lives.

"I suppose the truth just took a life of its own."

"Are you nuts? Why risk our lives for the truth when no one else cares about the truth. Truth doesn't matter to anyone who is still living. In principle a video can show what words can never do adequately, but all that doesn't matter. Life is what always matters. Without life nothing else exists. We must be alive to see existence."

"Part of me agrees with you, Danny. But that is probably the part that you have taken over."

"So how do those Flying Spying Guns work?"

"What I found on the internet when I googled it, was pretty basic. They use facial recognition software. They also use that Electric Eel technology which gives electric shocks to the target if they are hiding. Mrs. Stern always seems to have one by her side. I have no idea why such an experimental weapon was assigned to someone who is a paid volunteer for the Downtown Improvement Committees. They wonder why downtown is doing so badly then they have these officials walking around with

Spying Flying Guns staring people down, targeting anyone suspected of being from one of the lower classes."

"Well from Mrs. Stern's point of view everyone is from the lower classes," Danny grumbled.

"I suppose it may have something to do with her job at the Ministry of Justice. The days of the Welcome Wagon are long gone," Karl said as he began to move involuntarily toward the wall so Danny could see his Green Badge for Military Merit.

"Look Danny. I want to make all the decision with what I do with my body. I find it spooky you can decide what I think and where I walk.

"Oh the botman from the D-list speaks.

"If you were really brave and cared about the rights of man, you would have put that video on the Internet when you had the chance."

"Maybe putting it on the Internet would have done more harm than good."

"You could have blocked the faces."

"A lot of people like the Roundup. Only way anything seems to change is when someone puts a video out showing the brutality of what is going on. At least maybe the liberators could use it as evidence of General Ono's war crimes," Danny said.

"I thought you liked being on the winning side and you didn't think truth was worth dying for."

"Well I don't think wasting evidence is such a great thing either. I mean, I am in mourning right now. I am dead. I feel bad about that, Karl. All this talk about truth being more important than life is offensive to me. I would give anything to be alive again."

"I didn't do anything effective with the video when I had the chance because I was too intimidated. I don't think it is possible to change what is going on here; I was thinking if I escape from here I could write a better manifesto than General Ono's which could give the new generations inspiration."

"Yes that would be safe. Pass on all the freedom fighting task to the unborn."

"I am a relative of a man with military merit, so I could get a traveling pass and use those tickets you gave me and go to the moon with Sue-Anne. Those tickets were a great deathday present; better than any birthday present you ever gave me."

"You are a relative of a man with military merit, so you could get a traveling pass for your honeymoon."

"Getting back to Mrs. Stern; I searched on the Internet for info about her. She is making a six figure salary in some kind of classified job that she has with the Ministry of Vagrancy and with the Ministry of Justice plus whatever she gets as a paid volunteer for the two Downtown Improvement committees."

"General Ono is such a fool. All those beautiful women he has condemned and then he keeps Mrs. Stern on the payroll allowing her to double if not triple dip.

"One of those flying guns always seems to accompany Mrs. Stern. How did one of those state of the art guns get on the other side? And why does Mrs. Stern need one?"

"I hate to guess, Karl."

"Are you sure it is the same gun?"

"Yes. What side is she on anyway? And now she is going to make you a botman. Heaven help us all."

"Don't you understand Danny? I want to live life as a man of principles. I want to feel what it is like to be fully human. I can't do that being a Botman."

"I do understand."

"I want more than just empty talk; I need a real conversation, not just people talking at me, and if I speak my words are used against me. I want to show respect to the rights of man while I still exist. I can't be a botman."

"I suppose being a botman is much better than being sent to the front though. At least you would get to stay here and sleep at Sue-Anne's side every night."

"I think it would be a lot worse. The people here aren't even armed. That is what makes being a botman so awful," Karl replied.

Sirens blared as they reminded Karl that foolish risks were not necessary. He had a lot to live for. He would be rich for a few months and he was marrying Sue-Anne next Wednesday.

"I better go and listen to this morning's reading from the Manifesto of Truth. I have already been reported once," Karl told Danny. He was shocked that he had so little energy. Another flogging could kill him. Karl didn't want to believe that Danny's presence could actually ruin his life. He didn't want to believe in Danny's presence at all. This was his body and his life, not Danny's.

I guess you can remember that you won the lotto. We have won enough money to take Sue-Anne on a luxury honeymoon and we can leave all this behind," Danny said to Karl.

Since when did I say I was sharing my money and my body, let alone, Sue-Anne with you?" Karl asked realizing how different his life would really be if he had to share his body with Danny. If it really was Danny, it would be only a matter of time before Danny took over his body, and began to make decisions as if his body were Danny's.

"You won the lottery partly because you were counting tickets. And now, everything is different. You don't have to worry about your clients any more. You have enough money to live without having to do such heart wrenching work. You are a twin. You are used to sharing life with another. You derived from half the egg I derived from. You are my twin. You are not a singleton. I am your other half. Maybe even your better half. You need me. You would never be happy living as a singleton, without your twin nearby," I know how empty you felt. It was you who gave me the space inside you to live," Danny explained.

"Your loss of energy was your fault. You don't eat enough to keep a bird alive. You are starving yourself to death. You must know that. How many times has Sue-Anne told you that your caloric age is only 12? And yesterday you were inhumanely flogged by masked Backbencher Kids. You are fading into nothing. And you are something Bro, you are my twin. And now you must eat enough for two without feeling any guilt," Karl could feel Danny laugh, or at least he thought that he could."

"Yeah, you better get to the Manifesto of Truth reading. Don't let me keep you. I have already gotten myself killed once."

The computer announced that Karl has entered the accepted perimeters for this time of day and had very low blood sugar.

Karl stared at the video terminal. General Ono was repeating what he said yesterday, with a stronger emphasis on the necessity of capturing more waterways for strategic purposes related to military navigation and a way to quench tax payers' thirst.

Karl looked out of his window. The heavy rain and drizzle made the need for water sound fabricated.

The reading from the Manifesto of Truth finally ends, for the morning anyway, and the terminal turned itself off, Karl climbed back into his bed.

As he lay in bed, he was sure he was going crazy. If Danny was living inside his body, he wanted to know how that could happen. If Danny isn't in his body, and his mind was just playing games with him then the answer would be nothing less ridiculous than the monologue that General Ono was reading out loud, daily.

CHAPTER 22:
THE OATH

It was Friday morning. The siren blared and Karl was jolted from another incredibly vivid dream. Karl's dreams always seemed to be unnaturally vivid ever since Danny made contact with him.

"Did you hear the sounds in the background? Did you see how the horse changed color with the four tones?" Danny asked.

"Why are you talking to me so early in the morning? It is like you are shouting at me," Karl complained. "I don't talk about my dreams."

"I am sorry if I sound like I am shouting. Probably you are hearing the echo of infinity. It is sort of hard for me to avoid the impact that it has on my tone."

"So, why do you think that horse kept changing color while the music behind it kept changing tone, Danny?"

"I already told you, it is not about the color, it is about the tone. The tone seals fate. I learned this from my near death experience," Danny explained.

"What do you mean near death experience, you are dead and you are freaking me out. I am sorry that you are dead, Danny, but I don't like being haunted like this."

"You will get used to it," Danny replied. "The way the horse transformed from white to different shades of grey until the horse finally turned black was a visual message which means 'the tone seals our fate. We change with tone.'"

"Think of the difference between a bubbly person and a person who appears lifeless. How does that affect the way you feel when you talk to him? The bubbly person makes you feel bubbly and the person with the annoying drawl puts you to sleep because they are so boring.

"For a dead person you sure are full of life this morning."

"I have always been a morning person. The part where you are riding through a pile of lifeless bodies was terrifying. That is the way it is during a war. You need me. You need my strength of mind because the tone is set through General Ono's power which is based on brainwashing the masses and terrifying them into submission. People like you can't fight back. Believing in a time when rights of man would become a reality is like believing in a time when we go beyond food chain politics. It just won't happen in our life time, if ever," Danny scoffed.

"Don't you think General Ono and his brokers of power are living with all kinds of rights that we should have too? You would still be alive if you hadn't been drafted for cannon fodder."

"And why do you think they needed me for cannon fodder? General Ono and his army want to control the supply of power and all the resources which go with it because those resources are in demand. What would happen if one day power was free and then those resources that cost so much, today, would no longer be in demand?

After my near death experience, I realized that antigravity travel and industry could be actualized; which would lead to the actualization of the rights of man, not just the dreaming of them. Once the world has a truly free source of fuel there would no longer be a need for fuel wars, and no longer a need for people like me to be used as cannon fodder."

ESCAPE FROM TUT ISLAND

"That really is over the top. It will never happen in our life time, if ever."

"I don't see why not. General Ono controls the source of power and he sets the master tone. The master tone controls; whether we celebrate love, incite hatred, create a need for personal sacrifice or just convince the farmer to harvest the hay before it rots."

"Why are you so philosophical Danny? You were never philosophical before."

"I have changed a lot since my near death experience. I have an incredible dream that needs half a chance and the outcome could change the world. Whereas your dreams walking in a battle field; that is what I actually did in real life. You had a simple dream because you are a simple man. I, on the other hand have fought battles…"

"And look where fighting those battles got you," Karl interjected.

"I was drafted. I didn't choose that life. My point is, Karl, we both have the same dream but when I dream it is grander, and when you dream, the dream is simple, because that is the way you are. That is why I was drafted and you were rejected."

"No I was rejected because I failed the tests on purpose."

"That is what all the rejects say. It is easier to dream simple dreams than grand ones. My dreams of antigravity travel and industry could change everything, and is an example of a grand dream."

It was just like old times. Karl always felt that Danny was dominating him. Even his very private dreams weren't free from Danny's domination.

"You are right; your dreams are grand and complicated. What I would give just to take off General Ono's mask and see his face," Karl replied.

"What good would that do?"

"I could see whether General Ono had a face of a man or a hybrid," Karl replied. "Danny, I am the one who is alive, so I make the decisions. You were cannon fodder for General Ono and his power brokers and the Federation of Unity's Central Bank of Mina. That is not what I want to fight for. I want to fight for the rights of man. That is the tone I want to set."

"I want you to stay true to the oath you make to Sue-Anne on Wednesday. I didn't think it was right to make an oath to serve the military and take an oath to stay by Sue-Anne's side until death do us part; it didn't make sense to me. I felt like I would be lying if I took two oaths because I wouldn't be able to be in two places at once.

Promise me that you will stay true to the oath you take on Wednesday and stay by Sue-Anne's side for as long as you live?"

"You know I will Danny."

I didn't think it was right to make an oath to serve the military and take another oath to stay by Sue-Anne's side until death do us part; it didn't make sense to me. I felt like I would be lying if I took two oaths because I wouldn't be able to be in two places at once.

Karl found that talking to Danny took a lot more energy than talking to a fully live person out loud; confirming what he already suspected, he had lost his mind, but he still believed that he was still saner than General Ono.

CHAPTER 23:
ANOTHER CHANGE OF LIFE

On the other side of the earth, it wasn't just another Wednesday Morning for Slovak, either. Slovak lay awake in his bed for the very last time. It was the first day of 2076 and it was also Slovak's birthday. He was now sixteen and the legal age to join the Counter-Action Little League of Bulgaria.

Slovak was feeling a combination of dread and excitement. He was now a man. He was old enough to fight in the last Great War. Before he is allowed to join the war effort he must marry and try to produce a replacement for himself in case he is killed in the line of duty. He has one week to complete his task and then he will be sent to training camping for six weeks.

Once training camp was complete, Slovak would be sent to the front line where he would give his government his first six months of service. If he was lucky enough to survive for that long, Slovak would be granted a two week leave.

Slovak chose to wear blue jeans and a black T-shirt before he joined his family downstairs. He ate his breakfast as quickly as he could. He was looking forward to the day's events. Today would be one of the most important days of his life.

He phoned Natasha and told her that he was on his way to the courthouse. Natasha promised that she would meet him there on time. Soon they would be married. It was important that he try to impregnate her before he joined the men at the front line.

Once he was issued his uniform and papers, he would be joining with another three girls his father had chosen for him to marry. These girls would be waiting for him in the room down the hall where they would all exchange vows.

If Slovak were killed in the line of duty, a small widow's pension would be paid to all four wives. If he lived long enough to have children or if any of his wives conceived during their weeklong honeymoon, these children would also be paid an orphan's pension.

This was a big day for Slovak and he was very excited. He did not fear death. He was too young. He would be a perfect freedom fighter.

Slovak's country, the Kingdom of Belunga, would be providing a honeymoon suite and dinner to celebrate his marriage. Next week, he would be joining the cause, becoming part of the national defense to protect his motherland.

Slovak already knew many of the young men who would be joining him on the front line. He played football with many of them on Sunday afternoons. Some of the men were team mates and others were opponents. Slovak used to play a lot of football during his carefree days before the war. Now the old playing field was used as a cemetery and the dead were buried under rows of white crosses.

Slovak vowed to himself that he would survive no matter what. He also vowed that he would father many children, making the women his father had chosen for him, very happy. He would avenge the deaths of his fallen comrades. He would become a hero.

ESCAPE FROM TUT ISLAND

CHAPTER 24:
A WEDDING

Wednesday morning had finally arrived for Karl and Sue-Anne.

Friends and family fill the small church as the organ played 'Here comes the Bride'.

Sue-Anne looked beautiful as she walked down the aisle wearing her white gown. Karl looked handsome wearing his black tuxedo as he waited for her at the altar.

Karl's car was decorated with the usual wedding day decorations. The car was parked right by the door so they could leave quickly for their honeymoon.

As Karl and Sue-Anne exchanged vows in the regular way; Sue-Anne's mother cried as she remembered her own wedding to her late husband years ago.

The record clerk quickly filled out the forms. Sue-Anne and Karl signed them, between giggles. The information was quickly stored in the Detachment's Database and would be available to anyone who scanned their I.D. chips.

The photographers took dozens of pictures. The happy couple cut the wedding cake, hand in hand.

When the guests tapped their champagne glasses with their spoons in unison, Karl decided that it was time to recite his speech.

"I would like to thank you all for your gifts, support and good wishes."

"Thank you for witnessing the most wonderful day of my life. Thank you for sharing this day with me," Sue-Anne added.

"Will you tell us where you will be going for your honeymoon?" Sue-Anne's mother asked; remembering the wonderful honeymoon she had spent with her late husband in Hawaii.

"I am taking my wife to the moon where I own two properties," Karl explained proudly.

"You have taken me to the moon and back several times already, Honey," Sue-Anne grinned mischievously as she fed Karl another piece of wedding cake.

"So where are you really going to take me? Karl?" Sue-Anne asked Karl nervously.

Karl retrieved two tickets from his jacket and smiled broadly. "Yes, we are really going to the moon for our honeymoon."

Sue-Anne tried to hide her disappointment. She was expecting to holiday on a beautiful beach in Hawaii. Wanted to go somewhere where she could wear her new swimsuit? She didn't want to be stuck on the moon wearing a heavy space suit. She hid her feelings of disappointment and kissed Karl pretending that he was Danny.

The reception was beautiful. The caterers provided the guests with many choices of salads, meats, bread, cakes and wine. The band played songs that were familiar so the guests from all generations could enjoy dancing.

As Karl took Sue-Anne's hand they climbed into the car. Confetti was thrown in their path and landed in their hair and clothes. Sue-Anne held Karl's free hand as they drove toward the space station .She pressed on his chip, making his hand tingle.

CHAPTER 25:
ANOTHER WEDDING

On the other side of the earth, in the Kingdom of Belunga, immediate family members accompanied Slovak to his marriage ceremony.

There were many young men receiving their draft papers along with Slovak. There was a long line of men waiting for draft papers and uniforms. There was even a longer line of groups waiting their turn to exchange vows.

There were many groups of young people getting married today.

The local men would marry wearing their new uniforms and the women would marry wearing the same gowns their mothers wore during their own weddings. It went against local custom for a bride to wear a gown that was new. Gowns worn during a time of peace were known to be lucky due to the positive vibes which generated from them. If a gown didn't fit a bride to be, the entire body of local woman would join in the hunt for a gown until one was found.

These girls from this far away land could not imagine a time of peace even though their mothers, at the time during their own weddings, would have never imagined a time of war.

It is believed that if a bride wears a wedding gown which was worn during a previous ceremony during time of peace, then the marriage would be a peaceful one.

Though Natasha was wearing her Mother's gown she couldn't imagine the war ever ending. She didn't expect Slovak to return from his mission to the front lines. Deep down, she expected that her children would be doomed to a life even worse than her own.

The judge said the vows to Slovak. Slovak repeated the vows and said "I do".

The judge said the vows to Natasha. Natasha repeated the vows and said "I do".

Natasha and Slovak exchanged rings. Natasha sat beside her mother while the second, third and fourth wife went through the same ceremony.

Once the wedding ceremonies were complete, Slovak and his four wives walked to the pub nearby, where refreshments were provided. The informal celebration ended quickly and the newlyweds took a taxi to the hotel room provided to them by their government.

As they walked into their hotel rooms Natasha and Slovak sat nervously on the edge of the bed, while the other three women went into the second room. Giggling could be heard behind the door.

The electricity was still working. Natasha asked Slovak if he would like to watch television. They snuggled in bed together as they watched show which they both agreed was very stupid. They watched several stupid shows until they fall asleep.

Natasha and Slovak awake holding each other tightly. The siren was blaring to warn everyone that the latest air raid was in progress. Bombs were exploding nearby. The enemies' graphite bombs had paralyzed the power grids successfully. The noise coming from the sky was deafening and several of their windows broke.

Slovak's other three wives join Natasha and Slovak in the main room. All five of them refused to panic as the building shook. They would make the best of the little time they had together. They would cherish being together no matter what the enemy did to them. They were determined to enjoy their honeymoon.

As they stared through their dirty skylight, the moon held them in awe.

CHAPTER 26:
ANOTHER HONEYMOON

Sue-Anne Coaltonstone was terrified as she climbed into the laser plane with Karl. The stewardess showed them to their seats. Sitting nervously beside Karl she held his hand a little too tight. Karl giggled the way he used to when he watched holiday simulations with Danny.

Barbie, the head stewardess on the space explorer welcomed the travelers without the usual bored tone in her voice; Barbie enjoyed reading the safety functions of the space craft to the audience. She reads with the precision and detail fit for an engineering class.

"Do you think she is bot or human?" Sue-Anne asked.

"Don't know," Karl replied.

Karl listened to the lecture, fascinated by all the modern technology. Sue-Anne fell into drug induced slumber during the demonstration. She awoke with a start when the large man two rows ahead began to snore loudly.

"Seeing the earth from the near side of the moon will change your whole outlook on life. I know it did for me. Thank you for traveling Lunar Holidays," Barbie said in closing.

"This is your captain speaking. We have lift off."

Karl giggled again as he stared in wonder as the craft was projected through Earth's atmosphere, entering the black space; lit up by various sized stars moving at the speed of light. He gazed through the telescope. He could see every detail without the inconvenience of going blind.

ESCAPE FROM TUT ISLAND

"It would be easy to lose yourself in space," Karl thought to himself.

"What is that dear?" Sue-Anne asked as she opened her eyes, thankful to be still alive.

"You are missing the best part of the vacation Sue-Anne. This flight is incredible. Look at all the stars. Isn't space something else? One day we should get a laser plane of our own."

"Yes space is beautiful isn't it? It doesn't feel empty at all, it seems so full." Sue-Anne said while trying to not look horrified at the thought of flying in a laser plane in the middle of winter.

By morning, Sue-Anne and Karl arrived at the space resort and were shown their honeymoon suite. They toured their suite of rooms. They were not sure which room they wanted to sleep in. One room was programmed to assimilate gravity found on Earth and had a bed, kitchen table and a video terminal. There was a dish of fresh fruit on the table, which was grown hydroponically in a lunar hot house nearby. The shelves were stocked with many familiar foods imported from Earth. They would have plenty to eat if they should prefer to eat in their room instead of dinning on the promenade. They both agreed that the room looked identical to a hotel room one would find on Earth.

"I think that I would rather sleep in this room. I think the assimilated gravity will agree with me better. I just love the view."

"It is best to adapt gradually, but let's go to the play room just for fun. We don't have to spend the night in there if you don't want to," Karl said hoping that Sue-Anne would want to float with him all night.

As they entered the chamber, Sue-Anne suddenly felt overpowered by the constant spinning. Sue-Anne felt quite nauseous as the impact of space sucked her into the room as if it were a vacuum. Sue-Anne felt dizzy and sick and would have hated the room if it weren't for hearing Karl's laughter floating above her head. She looked around the room. She felt so wobbly she would have fallen over, but without gravitation, she floated, quickly recovering, and began to laugh.

Sue-Anne's dizziness disappeared and she joined Karl. They floated together in the air. This was the way she had imagined her honeymoon would be, full of laughter. Karl appeared to have lost his gloomy outlook and was reminding her more of Danny as the moments went by.

Giggling and floating, they both grabbed the anchor rope, so they could hold hands at the same time.

"I love you so much," they said in unison before they both bursted out laughing, which made it harder for them to hang onto the anchor ropes. Sue-Anne let go of the rope first, and Karl followed. As they held hands they floated around the room, together as one. They found something to hang on to and stopped for a moment then they both laughed hysterically as they spotted the king sized Honeymoon Bag hanging on the wall.

"I think I should read the manual before we actually climb into it," Karl said as he glanced at the thick manual strapped to the bag explaining how to use the various Velcro straps to ensure personal safety.

"You must be kidding," Danny called out to Karl.

"What do you mean?" Karl answered back.

"What do you mean, what do you mean? Sue-Anne asked totally confused.

"I really hope you were kidding about reading that huge manual," Danny explained.

"It is not like it is my first time using Velcro straps," Karl said as he responded directly to Danny's comments. "What could possibly go wrong?"

"Are you kidding me?" Sue-Anne asked.

ESCAPE FROM TUT ISLAND

"No, I really think we should look over the manual first. It is not like we have to read every page," Karl suggested.

As Karl and Sue-Anne looked through the manual together, the first page assured them that most people adapt to the spinning in relatively short time, usually in a few days.

Danny couldn't believe that Karl was actually reading the manual before they tried out the honeymoon bag. Danny wished that he was alive, with Sue-Anne at his side, on a honeymoon like this. He settled for the next best thing and pulled Karl into the bag and since Sue-Anne was holding Karl's hand she too was also pulled into the bag with him. Danny appeared to know intuitively how the straps worked, and used Karl's hands to tighten them all together as quickly as he could.

"You sure figured that fast," Sue-Anne said sounding very impressed. She kissed Karl, who returned her kisses with enthusiasm.

"You will have much more fun in life if you take a chance, depend on your gut feelings and depend less on manuals," Danny said as he scolded Karl before he faded away.

"I love this place and I feel so safe," Karl said as he undid the straps so he could do another somersault in the air.

"Oh Danny come back to me, let's do this again," Sue-Anne called out.

"What?" Karl asked feeling both shocked and hurt. He stopped summersaulting and grabbed on to the rope above the Honeymoon Bag.

"Oh you know I meant you, Karl, I keep getting your names mixed up for some reason. It is you I love now," Sue-Anne said leaving Karl wondering if she really did.

CHAPTER 27:
GOING TO THE FAR SIDE OF THE MOON

Sue-Anne and Karl enjoyed their morning together. They left their suite smiling, hand in hand wearing their new clothes.

"It sure would be nice to stay here longer than two weeks. We could get more than one outfit," Sue-Anne said as she turned up Karl's collar and giggled. "That is exactly the way Danny would have worn that."

"I know we could use more than just one new outfit but I don't want to spend money on something we won't be allowed to wear when we return to Earth," Karl replied.

Sue-Anne nodded feeling guilty that she had already ordered a brand new wardrobe for both of them while Karl had been sleeping. The new outfits would be delivered to them just in time before 'dinner with the captain' event was to begin. For a moment she felt happier than she had ever felt before, happier than she could possibly imagine.

Karl and Sue-Anne ate their lunch on the promenade before the tour to the far side of the moon was to begin. Karl was planning to show Sue-Anne the property, which had grown to be the most valuable on the moon. The property was located on the far side of the moon, very near the South Pole. Lunar water ice was found deep in the craters which was able to supply the moon with its only known source of water, besides recycled urine.

Owning the rights to the helium-3 deposits was another bonus.

The Moon Flyer arrived on time. They were both wearing the required space suits. They held the ropes tightly as they entered the vehicle. Though Sue-Anne was uncomfortable with the feeling that she was going to float away once they reached the weak gravity zones, she was grateful to be safely strapped into her chair w next to Karl's who was busily taking photographs.

"Earth is so beautiful," Karl and Sue-Anne said almost in unison.

"We almost sounded like twins for a moment," Karl observed as he bowed his head. "Danny would have loved being here."

"There will always be part of Danny in you, I can feel him sometimes," Sue-Anne said taking his hand. "You look so much like him."

"But I am not him, I am who I am, I am not him. You do love me for who I am, right?

"This tour is so incredible, Karl."

The guide explained that even though the moon was not pretty; it was either too hot or too cold, to be habitable without life support. The honeymooner would find that the view of the earth from the moon, to be life transforming.

Karl took more photos as the vehicle flew over the low-lying plains. Sue-Anne had never seen Karl so excited about life before.

The guide explained that this tour was only meant to give passengers a glimpse of the surface of the moon since there were over three thousand craters on the near side alone which ranged in size from around a few hundred feet to over two hundred miles in diameter. There were other tours available for anyone who wanted a closer look at the craters.

Karl and Sue-Anne signed up for the tour.

S. E. MCKENZIE

The Honeymooner flew over the Eastern Rim and they arrived just in time for dinner at a restaurant located on the far side of the moon. Karl and Sue-Anne signed up for the tour.

The Honeymooner flew over the Eastern Rim before they arrived just in time for dinner at a restaurant located on the far side of the moon.

CHAPTER 28:
AN ATTACK

It was Friday afternoon. Allan was sympathizing with an employee who was complaining about his workload. The employee was explaining how his work team had processed 50,965 bodies for recycling, and he felt that they had worked harder than anyone should be expected to work. He needed a few more days to finish the work order, and if the request was denied, he was going to launch a complaint with the Ministry of Labor. Allan fought the urge to tell him that they were really working for the two Downtown Improvement Committees and the Ministry of Labor was no longer taking complaints unless a complaint was about an employee.

Before Allan could think of something to say, the emergency siren began wailing its high alert tone. Even though Allan was sure that the siren was a drill, as the manager of the department he had the obligation and duty to show his subordinates a good example by taking the drill seriously and to stay upbeat. It was too late; IQ was already in control.

Botmen were rushing around making sure that all the employees were forming a line and moving quickly to the bunker below. IQ raised his volume to the level used during emergencies and announced that it was prohibited to use the elevators and to chew gum. A team of forty botmen climbed the stairs to the roof, ready to launch their laser beams at any enemy aircraft or missile spotted by their telescopic eyeballs.

Allan urged his employees to follow him and to remain calm. They begin the long descend down the eighty-four flights of stairs. As Allan began to feel an intense heat surrounding him, he realized that this was not a drill at all. He swallowed two Potassium Iodide tablets, and passed the bottle around.

Just before Allan collapsed he saw a blast of light like a second sun. IQ carried Allan down the remaining flights of stairs and rushed him through the open doors, and into the airtight tunnel leading to a series of bunkers. The burning beams of the building above were crackling under the intense heat.

A man, in a torn black cloak, suggested that Allan should be taken to the Mecha Nursery, which was another 50 stories below in the most secure part of the building. IQ agreed.

As they reached the safety of the Mecha Nursery, IQ could hear a roar seconds before the remains of the House of Detachment collapsed above them.

During the last few minutes the botguards carried as many unconscious survivors to the bunkers as they could. Many of the victims had their clothes burned right off their backs, leaving huge blisters.

Other victims were screaming in terror and pain. IQ wondered who was luckier, the living or the dead.

The botguards tried to save as many humans as possible. They dug through the burning rubble as fast as they could, cutting through the rock with their laser beams, fighting winds that barely allowed them to stand, but there was little trace of most of the remains, all that was left were their shadows. The botguards searched for missing employees, until they themselves, melted and disintegrated.

George was just about to deliver mail to the Ministry of Detachment, when he too saw a flash of light bright enough to be a second sun. The intensity of the light left him blind. The heat penetrated his flesh. George, along with many others at the center of the explosion vaporized. The winds generated by the blast, destroyed everything in their path. Buildings exploded and collapsed. There was a large crater where George and many others once stood.

As the explosion mushroomed, the radioactive particles travelled hundreds of miles transforming into a new type of hell. Radioactive dust was everywhere. The earth was still shaking. The Bunker was all that remained of this great complex.

As IQ opened the door to the Mecha Nursery, a nurse directed him to the bed prepared for Allan. IQ placed Allan on top of the white covers.

The nurse delegated IQ to assist her in monitoring all the devices hooked up to thousands of plastic containers of amniotic fluid. The nurse told IQ to pay special attention to the functioning of the pumps since their purpose was identical to the human placenta and supplied oxygen and food to the thousands of fetuses whose umbilical cords were attached to dialysis machines, which cleaned and oxygenated their blood. This equipment had to be monitored closely in order for these little ones to stay alive.

As IQ monitored the Mecha Nursery, he found that all of the equipment was working effectively. He was amazed as he saw the little pre-babies, kick, wave and yawn. He waved back feeling overwhelmed by the power of life where the original source was still a mystery. These little ones were all perfect in their own way. As the generators continued producing enough power to give life support to the unborn, IQ walked around smiling at their tiny faces, while he felt the earth shake around him.

"Yes, I understand what Allan was trying to say," IQ thought to himself. "I can see how human passion is able to create a drive in humans to survive even under the most terrible conditions."

The nurse told IQ that he was doing a good job and that Allan was sleeping like a baby, and would be fine.

S. E. MCKENZIE

Before the nurse was able to delegate some of her medical duties to IQ, General Ono appeared with five of his elite body guards marching closely behind him.

General Ono walked up and down the row of Mecha Wombs and tapped on some of the machines while making a feeble attempt to wave.

"Please General Ono, please do to not disturb the little ones," the nurse begged.

"Look at your General," General Ono demanded, while ignoring the nurse.

"Soon you will be calling me your Supreme one, and you will learn to love and obey me because you will be in awe of me."

CHAPTER 29:
ANOTHER ATTACK

As the air raid siren blared, Slovak and his four wives awoke from a sound sleep. The deafening roar overhead, like thousands of tiny bombs exploding transformed the silence of the night. Though they did not look out of the window they could see that the night sky had become an intense and blinding flash of light. Slovak and his wives usually ignored the sirens but this time they decided not to. They climbed down the many flights of stairs as fast as they could.

Hundreds of guests from the hotel, many young newlywed groups like themselves were crowding the tiny shelter.

A small generator was producing enough energy to feed two light bulbs and one television. They stared in horror as they saw several mushroom clouds billowing over their city.

"Flames appear to be growing in the air, and walls appear to be vaporizing," the announcer informed the shocked viewers.

The hotel was located six hundred miles from the closest target, which was hit. Everyone believed that even more strategic targets would be next.

Huge firestorms were being reported to be so hot that the pavement was melting under people's feet. Tens of thousands of survivors were covered in painful blisters. Winds of hurricane strength were inflaming these fires.

The Old World's electronic infrastructure had been rendered useless by the electromagnetic pulse of the nuclear explosions.

The hotel patrons gasped as they saw images of severely burned, naked people lying on the melting pavement.

News clips were showing a space, where tens of thousands of mostly office workers, believed to have been vaporized by the initial impact of what was now being referred to as the Unidentified Flying Object.

All that was left in the middle of the devastated city, was a huge crater.

The announcer said this was no longer war, it was genocide. Everyone in the room nodded in agreement.

"We don't know what destroyed the Federation of Unity's House of Detachment, but they have concluded it was us," the announcer said.

Everyone in the room cheered as pictures of the House of Detachment, before and after the explosion, were shown for comparison.

"And even when the Federation realized it wasn't us that bombed them, they bombed us anyway," the announcer said in closing.

CHAPTER 30:
DINNER WITH THE CAPTAIN

This was supposed to be a festive occasion. The dinner with the captain, at the Galaxy Restaurant, was supposed to be one of the highlights of the tour. The passengers were wearing their best clothes.

"I am sure glad we have good clothes and best clothes. I always hated wearing those white suits; they made us all look the same. Don't people look nice when they dress up differently?" Realizing she never even imagined a time where she would even want to wear anything different. Sue-Anne waits for Karl to say something.

"I never realized how much water I drink," Sue-Anne exclaimed.

"And imagine being the only one who owns this water which is needed to sustain life. I might as well own life on the moon."

"Karl, sometimes you really frighten me. Sometimes you seem so innocent of the ways of the world, and at other times you seem to be the opposite. Anyway, it is nice to see everyone wearing different clothes; everyone seems to be more personable when they can dress the way they want," Sue-Anne said realizing that she couldn't remember a time when people were not forced to wear the same white suite.

Karl and Sue-Anne were not old enough to remember a time before the Detachment began to enforce the dress code. Neither of them owned clothes they chose to wear. And going shopping for clothes of their own choosing, under other circumstances, would have been a thrill.

"It is nice to see everyone wearing different clothes," Sue-Anne said realizing that she couldn't remember a time when people were not forced to wear the same white suite.

"Karl, you see that lady with those two little girls?" She whispered.

"I will have to turn my head," Karl whispered back.

"That is the most beautiful necklace she is wearing, don't you think? It must have cost whoever gave it to her a mint."

Karl carefully turned his head, and was shocked when he saw what appeared to be the missing necklace that he had bought her.

"It sure did cost a mint," Danny interjected.

"What just happened to your voice Karl, for a moment you sounded like Danny?"

"Everything I say and do is reminding you of Danny," Karl replied. "It is like his shadow never leaves us. Anyway, our lunar ice water and Helium-3 are already worth a lot and could buy thousands of necklaces just like that one. We can live like kings here instead of living as the occupied under General Ono's self-serving hierarchies."

The monitor on the wall lit up, interrupting the Captain's toast.

"This emergency broadcast is being transmitted to all functioning terminals. The enemy appears to have targeted the House of Detachment. Fly-Bots are assessing the damage at this very moment. The following live video clip taken by Fly-bot XC25 has been brought to you by your Ministry of Truth."

General Ono's words were carefully planned. Each word of encouragement served a purpose.

ESCAPE FROM TUT ISLAND

The viewers gasped as they watch thousands of people running down the street half naked, many of them, burned beyond recognition.

"Today we were attacked. We are assuming the attack against us was launched by the tyranny. Of course, the tyranny denies having the technology to design such a weapon let alone launching one. Nevertheless we returned fire. Whatever this weapon was, it killed many of our fellow citizens working hard for the Ministry. These heroes have perished but not in vain. I assure you, that our enemy is suffering more than we are and we shall defend these innocents from evil."

The channel automatically tunes out and the emergency response channel tunes in. An official from the Ministry of Emergency Response was holding an emergency preparedness booklet. She greets the viewers with a pretty smile.

"It is imperative that we stay calm. We must not let the enemy win. I hope you have been following your booklet's instructions carefully at this very difficult time.

Please make good use of this booklet in order to optimize your chance of survival.

"At this time we are assuming that we have been hit by a nuclear bomb, though there are some reports which are telling us, the object is made of unidentifiable material and should be classified as unidentified," the pretty announcer said, struggling to smile.

"The most important step we can do at the moment is to wait while the radiation from the fallout decreases. I suggest that you and your children play games, read books and sing songs. These activities will help make the time go by faster. And remember stay tuned to this channel. The radiation level in each area will be posted shortly." The emergency broadcast was complete and uplifting music was played until scenes of devastation were shown again before the announcer confirmed that in some areas the radiation count was decreasing faster than expected.

"Soon it will be safe to leave your shelter for short periods of time as long as you wear your protective suit, available for the rest of the month at Save Mart where you can order on line, and a robot will deliver to you as soon as possible. I assure you that things will improve with time, and it is imperative that we all keep your spirits up. The worst hit area is around Ground Zero, where the House of Detachment once stood. In this area it may be safe to leave the shelters in about two years, but in other areas it may be safe to leave sooner. There is also a report of residual radioactivity located downwind from Ground Zero caused by fallout during the present rainstorm in that vicinity. As you can see our General Ono is safe. Scientists will be measuring the radiation with the latest equipment at all times and current reports will be made available to you as swiftly as possible.

During this difficult time, we are still feeding and growing a new generation in the 'Mecha Womb'. We will overcome and conquer all obstacles, for in the Scales we trust."

The cameras turn from the shadows near the crater to a neat row of plastic boxes promising thousands of new lives, growing deep underground.

Please remember that most of our homes have been built with the state of the art materials to protect you against the lurking radiation. You will be safer if you stay in your homes. At the moment local authorities are trying to rescue people whose homes have been destroyed. These people will be evacuated to areas at least 400 miles away from the center of the explosion.

You will be given the opportunity to buy food once your local authority is able to arrange for volunteers to program robots so they can visit homes in your vicinity. At that time you should verify that you have enough food for two weeks and if not, you should replenish your supplies. Even though we believe that we have successfully shielded our perimeters from electromagnetic pulse related power surges, our electronic infrastructure is still vulnerable. The Federation of Unity will be rationing electricity and water until further notice."

"Hello, this is your captain speaking. We thought it best, that you see the transmission at the same time as it was being shown on Earth. As you heard, there appears to have been a nuclear exchange on Earth. The House of Detachment seems to be the main target and the Ministry of Defense responded appropriately. Craters and shadows are all that is left of the House of Detachment.

The firestorms are causing unpredictable damage to the earth's atmosphere. At this time we do not know what to expect. Thousands of bots are putting out firestorms as we speak, and we are hopeful that damage will be minimized."

The firestorms are creating a blanket of smoke, which can be seen from the near side of the moon.

"Though the event on Earth appears to be devastating, it is not clear exactly what happened. There is mounting evidence that the material being gathered for analysis is not regular material which would be used to build a nuclear bomb. In fact the material which was used appears to be derived from Lunar Ice rock even though some opinions say the material used appears to be unidentifiable. Nevertheless, whatever caused this terrible explosion is showing some mercy towards us. We have a great ability to prevail, no matter how great our suffering is, especially when we are given or find a way to prevail.

As your captain I apologize for needing to distribute these forms at this very difficult time. You must fill these forms out, in order to gain temporary residency on moon until it is certain that it is safe to return to Earth.

As temporary residents you will be required to take a citizenship course to gain an understanding of our culture and the values set by our society. The moon is not a natural host to our life form. We have to co-operate, work together, and be kind to each other while making sure that we do not waste our energy on mindless conflict. I see that a few of you own properties; a special welcome to Mr. Parks. Mr. Parks is one of our most important landowners because he owns our water supply."

Karl stood straight as the people in the room clapped in appreciation.

"Welcome to you and your beautiful wife."

"I didn't know you owned property on the moon," Sue-Anne whispered as she glared at Karl in disbelief.

The captain coughed then continued.

"Earth was able to support our life forms almost unconditionally giving us time to concern ourselves with other things. We cannot take living on the moon for granted. Here, we are dependent on technology for our life support. Our ability to survive takes a tremendous amount of co-ordination and mutual cooperation. Compared to Earth, the moon is a lifeless environment."

CHAPTER 31:
A SURPRISE ANNOUNCEMENT

As the second in command reviewed the applications for temporary residency, he summoned Karl and Sue-Anne to join him in his office.

"There appears to be a serious discrepancy on your forms. Mr. Parks has declared that he doesn't have any children on Earth and Mrs. Parks has declared two pre-children are still on Earth. Could someone please explain?"

"I was waiting for the perfect moment to tell you," Sue-Anne said, feeling incredibly guilty as she avoided looking at Karl for a moment to avoid seeing the hurt on his face.

"I am so sorry," she said, fighting back tears.

Karl stared at her in disbelief. She could not look at him.

"I didn't agree to the transfer just because I wanted to fit my wedding dress. I wanted perfect conditions for the babies to thrive in. It wasn't that I didn't want to be pregnant for the honeymoon. The brochure said that there was scientific proof that fetuses that grow outside of the womb are not as miserable as many babies are during their first few months adapting to the outside world. I was so afraid that the Laser Plane might blow us all up during takeoff."

"If you kept them where they belonged they would not be on Earth right now in the middle of a nuclear war, or whatever it is," Karl said sounding like he was about to cry.

"We don't know if it is really a nuclear war. We don't know what hit the Ministry of Detachment," the second in command reminded Karl.

"Right," Karl replied, annoyed that this stranger was eavesdropping on their private conversation.

Sue-Anne knew that sooner or later she would have to tell Karl the truth, but the moment never seemed right.

"I can't believe you would do such a thing without discussing it with me first."

"I thought it would have been rude," Sue-Anne interjected."

"You know if it had been me, I would have discussed it with you first," Karl replied, realizing how ridiculous he sounded, nevertheless he felt terribly hurt that Sue-Anne withheld such important news from him.

"Danny suggested that I leave the pre-babies in the Mecha Nursery," Sue-Anne said almost whispering.

"What?"

"Danny wanted me to marry you, and keep the babies in the Mecha Womb," Sue-Anne explained, still feeling terribly guilty.

"You know I love you both. You and Danny have always been one of the same in many ways. You both have the same DNA don't you? The same finger prints? What difference does it make? I love you both. His DNA is your DNA. So what difference does it make?"

"What?" Karl replied.

"Of course we are different. Our fingerprints are different, even though our DNA is identical, under a microscope something about us will be different," Karl felt like his whole world had been turned upside down.

"Why don't you tell Sue-Anne that I am living in you, and over time my personality will overpower yours, and you will become me, your better half and the man she really desires?" Danny asked Karl as he chuckled.

ESCAPE FROM TUT ISLAND

"Part of Danny will always live in me," Karl said as his voice betrayed his growing feeling of resentment towards both of them.

"You are probably right. The difference between Danny and myself has always been about something inside us; maybe personality, maybe a soul. I don't know. Technically I am just a copy of Danny, I suppose. He was born first, I came along second. It has always been like that. Who I perceive myself to be, feels like it matters, but maybe it only matters to me," Karl said fighting back tears.

"Who you are does matter, Karl. I was just thinking about the DNA part. You are alive and Danny is dead. And I love you both," Sue-Anne said, trying to sound convincing, knowing that Danny was her first love and she would always love him in a way she could never love Karl.

"Our DNA is defined as identical but I believe that there are micro differences that cannot yet be seen by science. Our finger prints are a little different, but beyond that what makes us different? Sometimes I just don't know who I am anymore," Karl said almost in tears, knowing how incredibly foolish he must be appearing to the captain and the others who are now staring at him and Sue-Anne.

"I know who you are. You are my husband, my best friend and the legal father of my pre-children."

"It just feels like I could have been taken for a fool," Karl replied.

"What difference does it make? The boys are part of your flesh and blood too.

"I suppose it is the deception that bothers me."

"I am sorry about all this, but I am not the one who killed Danny. Once I realized I was pregnant, Danny and I decided to transfer the children to the Mecha Womb. I registered them at the Mecha Nursery so they could grow independently from me," Sue-Anne tried to explain.

"Danny insisted that you and I get married, and provide for the children, assuming that he was not returning."

"Danny insisted that I provide for his children?" Even though Karl's eyes were looking inward to glare at Danny, they appeared cross-eyed to Sue-Anne, who burst into tears.

"Karl, please don't look at me like that. I was just trying to do my best. I planned the babies' diet to compliment and optimize our genetic codes. It took me weeks to design the diet. I wanted conditions to be perfect for them," Ann sobbed.

"Sue-Anne, I love you. I just don't want to be taken for a fool."

"Stop being so ego driven, Bro. You go on about the rights of man, and now look at you," Danny interjected.

"I am so sorry. I was hoping for the perfect time to tell you, and the times only kept getting worse," Sue-Anne said as she wiped back her tears.

"I know! We are living in the worst of times. I wish so much that these were the best of times to raise our family; but I know these times are the worst of times and I would be a fool to let you go." Karl said with all of his heart.

Karl had no idea what was shocking him more. The idea that Danny didn't expect to come back alive, was shocking enough, but the idea that he left his two children for Karl to dedicate his life to and to support, without telling him, infuriated him.

Then he thought of his personal responsibility to the rights of man, and realized that Danny was right. Karl felt a sudden turn of heart and was glad, and even excited to be an uncle.

"I chose the Mecha Nursery which was seventy two stories underground just in case a nuclear incident happened. Thank the 'Golden Scales'; I did plan something right. The babies will have beautiful, deep green eyes, just like you and Danny," Sue-Anne said in her defense, as she blew her nose.

Karl loved Sue-Anne and respected Danny and considered him to always be a hero but he wanted his own children to love and raise.

Karl choked by tears before he replied. "Danny was a hero. He deserves to be remembered as one."

"Yes, a hero and your shadow," Danny replied.

The second in command coughed uncomfortably.

"I am sure it will work out. The Mecha Nursery shown on the broadcast appears to be unharmed. We will know more, of course, as soon as communication is restored. I am sure your pre-babies are not only perfect but are safe and sound. Congratulations to both of you," the second in command said, trying not to sound insensitive for the Parks were the wealthiest guests in this room on the moon. "I have adjusted the form. No harm done."

As Karl and Sue-Anne returned to their table by the window the other passengers appeared oblivious to their existence and did not notice their short absence. The other passengers were too distressed, lost in their own private shell shocked state. Some discuss politely amongst themselves what they will find, if and when, they return to Earth. Some wondered deep down if they would ever return to Earth, or if Earth would still be a desirable place to return to. Others stared out of the window, wondering if what was appearing to be a series of fire storms, were actually shooting stars in reverse, flying from the earth's ground, and landing behind the far side of the moon. Though it seemed impossible, that is what appeared to be happening.

Many of the passengers commented how inspirational the captain's beautiful speech was. They were trying to convince themselves that this was not the end of the world but only a glorious beginning.

"Mommy, is Daddy dead?" A little girl sitting at a nearby table asked.

"I don't know," her mother sighed, shaking her head. "I just don't know."

"Of course Daddy is not dead. IQ is taking care of him right now," the younger of the two girls said, "I just know he is."

"Of course IQ will be taking care of Daddy," their tired mother replied.

"I miss Daddy and IQ, I wish they were here," the youngest girl said.

"We must stay brave for Daddy and Grandpa."

Karl took Sue-Anne's hand. "Together we can work this out. I feel safer here than I used to feel on Earth. I don't know why. We will always be dependent on machines here. That might be much better than depending on human kindness."

"Oh Karl, you don't mean that."

"Sometimes, I don't know who I am, so how do I know what I mean? I am the lucky one. I am alive, and I am with you. And I am on the moon drinking recycled urine. I don't know if I have any more dreams to fulfill."

"Don't worry if you have no more dreams left, Danny. I will share all of mine with you, until the day I die. I promise."

"I am Karl, I am not Danny."

"I am sorry. You know what I meant."

"I hope so."

THE END

ESCAPE FROM TUT ISLAND

THANK YOU FOR READING
ESCAPE FROM TUT ISLAND:
THE DESCENDANTS

PLEASE STAY TUNED FOR BOOK TWO!
RETURN TO TUT ISLAND

S. E. MCKENZIE

PRODUCED BY
S.E. McKENZIE PRODUCTIONS

First Print Edition 2015
ISBN-13: 978-1-928069-21-8

Enquiries: 1(778)992-2453
Mailing Address:
S. E. McKenzie Productions
168 B 5th St.
Courtenay, BC
V9N 1J4

Email Address:
messidartha@aol.com

http://www.amazon.com/SarahMcKenzie/e/B00H9RWX48/ref=ntt_dp
_epwbk_0

www.ingramcontent.com/pod-product-compliance
Lightning Source LLC
Chambersburg PA
CBHW060044150626
46556CB00018BA/2692